D1136684

Nothing else Matters

FAIRMUIR
PARISH CHURCH

SUNDAY SCHOOL LIBRARY

F. 19

Patricia St. John

Nothing else Matters

SCRIPTURE UNION,
130 City Road, London EC1V 2NJ

Another *Swift* book by Patricia St. John
The Victor

© Patricia M. St. John 1982
Reprinted 1983, 1984

ISBN 0 85421 972 2

All Rights Reserved. No part of this publication may be
reproduced, stored in a retrieval system, or transmitted, in
any form or by any means, electronic, mechanical, photo-
copying, recording or otherwise without the prior permis-
sion of Scripture Union.

Printed and bound in Great Britain
at The Pitman Press, Bath

Introduction

This story is set in modern Lebanon, a land tragically affected by events in neighbouring Palestine. For many years the people of Lebanon were divided roughly into two communities, of almost equal size – half Christian, half Moslem – who had lived peacefully together, and had shared in the nation's prosperity and in the government of the country. But the emergence of the Jewish State to the south, and the resulting bitter conflict between Israel and the Palestinians, spilled over into Lebanon. The refugee camps were set up by the United Nations organisations and the Palestine Liberation Organisation movement grew within these camps. They have since established military training centres for commando activity.

In the end fighting broke out in 1958 and again in 1975 between the two parties, 'Christian' and 'Moslem', often described as 'right-wing' and 'left-wing' respectively, and this led to an exceptionally cruel civil war, only partially halted by the coming of the so-called Peace Force at the end of 1976. The labels 'Christian' and 'Moslem' can be misleading, for each party includes those who do not take their religion seriously or who have a very limited idea of what it means. Politics are at the root of the struggle, but the religious factor makes the conflict specially bitter and hard to resolve.

The majority of the Christians in Lebanon, including the principal characters in this book, belong to the Maronite church which is led by its own Patriarch, but is in communion with the Roman Catholic church. The Maronites are also a very strong political party, pledged to maintain the independence of Lebanon. They have their own militia and have formed the backbone of the resistance to other national and foreign forces which for years have been involved in the fighting in Lebanon.

In this book, the story of Moomi is fictitious, although many babies were found alive under their mother's bodies and some were happily adopted. Nearly all the other incidents are taken from the historical records of those months, or based on the true experiences of those who survived.

1

'Lamia, where is your brother?'

Sixteen-year-old Lamia started, for her father, always rather an aloof figure, had spoken more sharply than usual. He stood in the doorway, smartly dressed, brief-case in hand, and he wanted an answer at once.

Lamia laid down the basin of yoghurt she was eating and looked her father straight in the face.

'I don't know, Father,' she replied quietly. 'Maybe he went out early.'

'Nonsense! His bed has not been slept in, and don't lie to me, for I know that you know.'

'No, Father, I do not know where he is. But if he wasn't at home last night, then I think he would have slept in Hanni's house.'

'I see! Then they're both in it, are they? And you too!' His eyes flashed with anger. 'Fools, all of you, throwing away your lives for a few hours of excitement! Have you no thought for your mother? If you see him, tell him I have something to say to him – and don't be late for school.' He turned on his heel and was gone. A moment later they heard him slam the door of his Mercedes and drive out of the courtyard.

Eleven-year-old Sami and eight-year-old Huda looked curiously at their sister whose face had gone rather pale. They were sitting together having breakfast on the verandah under the great trellised vine which would soon sprout into leaf. They were eating yoghurt and olives and hot flaky bread, while the sun rose over the dip between the mountain peaks, bathing them in warmth and light.

'Where is Amin?' asked Sami bluntly. 'We know that you know and we want to know too. Has he gone fighting? Tell us!'

'If he's gone fighting it is better that you do not know, my son,' said their mother's voice behind them. She carried a tray of cups of coffee, and sat down beside them. 'Ai, Ai!' she mourned. 'And he so young and fine! At the sound of the gun they are like horses pawing for battle, these young men. War is in his blood; he will not obey us . . . and all for a fishermen's quarrel! We live in evil days.'

'No, Mother, not for a fishermen's quarrel! It's far, far greater than that. Every young man should be ready. But in any case, I am not fighting; I am only training.' Amin, too, had come through the house unnoticed and now stood in front of them. His face was weary and streaked with dirt, his arms stained with grease, but he laughed as he sat down and placed his arm round his mother's waist; and she laughed too, for this gay young son of hers was irresistible, and she could not spoil this moment with her displeasure.

'Go and wash at once,' she said, trying to speak sternly and not succeeding. 'You have just time to eat before the school bus arrives!' And she bustled off into the kitchen and poured all the love of her heart and a few tears into the omelette and coffee she prepared for him.

The little ones scampered off to collect their books and put on their overalls, but Lamia sat on, her dark eyes very grave, staring out over the mountain still shadowed. It was early April and the terraces rising from the town were a foam of blossom washed by the silver grey of the olive trees, with white villas rising above the luxuriance, tier upon tier all the way up the mountain. 'What a beautiful country it is!' she thought. 'It's all very well for fishermen to fight for their rights and refugees to fire guns, but it could never touch us. We are rich and safe and happy,' and she turned to smile at her brother who had come back, clean and ready for school, and was now wolfing his breakfast. They were alone and both very conscious of that oneness of spirit that exists between twins.

'I don't think it will be long,' said Amin suddenly, as though his thoughts had been hers, 'and I must be ready. When it comes, our heritage, our citizenship, and our Christian faith will all be at stake. Can't you make our parents understand? We shall all have a part to play.'

'Mother understands,' replied Lamia, 'but not Father. He wants you for the business and, besides, he thinks you are too young.'

'There will be no business unless we hold on. There are younger boys than me in the Moslem and Palestinian parties, training and in uniform. My friend Kamal, who lives on the edge of the camp, has a gun and knows how to use it.'

'A gun? Have you a gun, Amin?'

He laughed. 'Of course I have, little sister, or how should I train to fight? But it need not be mentioned. I leave it and my uniform at Hanni's house down the road. I had a few hours' sleep there this morning. I can see our bus coming. Is Sami ready?'

He picked up his school bag, went into the kitchen to kiss his mother, and strode down the garden path with Sami trotting behind. A few minutes later Lamia and Huda raced for the next bus, turning for a moment to wave at the gate.

They were gone, the four of them, out into this new threatening world, and their mother stood at the railing staring after them. She could not follow them even in thought; for she had come to the house eighteen years before, from a village, as the teen-age bride of a man she hardly knew, as the wedding had been arranged by her parents. But she had done her duty; she had become a superb housewife and borne his children, and, as a bonus, had learned to love her silent merchant husband. Apart from visits to the family and the church, she seldom went out except to the local shops, and she had found deep, creative contentment in the white house with its spacious garden. Happiness, to her, was the smell of bread baking, the fragrance of crushed wheat and fresh vegetables, the laughter of healthy, well-fed children round about her; and far above all other happiness, the nearness and gaiety of her son, Amin – her firstborn and the light of her eyes. Yes, life had been good to her, and when things went wrong there was always the crucifix on the wall. She thought it might be a good thing to kneel in front of it now, and her thoughts flew back to Amin again. He had found her looking up at it one day, and said in his loving, teasing voice:

'You're superstitious, Mother. How can that piece of wood help you?'

'It's not a piece of wood,' she replied, startled and shocked. 'It's the cross on which Jesus died, and I pray to him.'

The laughter died from his eyes, and he had stared sombrely at the pale, drained little figure. 'Always a dead Christ!' he had said at last. 'Can a dead Christ help us? Can that little wooden figure with nailed hands stop fighting and war?'

She had not been able to give him any convincing answer, but she had worried about him and gone secretly to the church on the hillside to light a candle for him and to pray in front of the big crucifix. Now she worried again and a cold fear seemed to clutch at her heart. She knew less about politics than her twins, but she did know that the fishermen's quarrel had not really been a small matter. A good man, who had championed the cause of the poor, had died of wounds; cars had been burned, and the great road south had been blocked by guns and flaming tyres. When the army had intervened, sixteen more had died in the clash, and on both sides there were hearts still burning with hate and revenge.

She discovered that she was trembling. Perhaps they could persuade Amin to pull out. After all, he was only sixteen, too young to be really involved. Surely the tide of violence could never reach their peaceful home, protected to the east by the Lebanon range and by the orange groves on the south.

But between the orange groves and the war-torn south lay those hotbeds of seething, wronged, exiled humanity, the Palestinian camps.

2

Sunday dinner was always a peaceful time. Rosa, Lamia and the two younger children usually went to Mass in the Maronite church up on the hill while Amin and his father slept off the exertions of the week, and at midday the whole family dined together on the verandah. It was the hour in the week that Rosa loved best, for no one was in a hurry and she could feed her whole family at once with the food that she had mostly prepared on Saturday, and she was therefore free to sit down and share in the general merriment and family discussions.

But today Amin would not be dining with them, much to Rosa's disappointment, for she always found herself cooking specially for him. He had unwillingly obeyed his father, and the local militia training corps had seen no more of him for the past week; but today his Party Leader was dedicating a new church west of the river. Amin seldom had an opportunity of actually seeing his hero but this Sunday he and Hanni would stand in the crowd, and perhaps the great man might glance in their direction and know, from their shining eyes and steadfast young faces, that two of his followers, at least, were ready to lay down their lives for the cause.

Amin went off quite early, carefully dressed for the occasion. He had blacked his shoes till they shone and his mother had pressed his suit till it looked like new. She was glad about this expedition because he seldom went near a church, and even his father's face relaxed in a proud little smile as his son bade him a respectful goodbye.

The morning passed quietly; Rosa sat on the verandah, chopping vegetables for lunch, the children played in the garden, and Lamia settled down to her homework; but somehow she could not concentrate. Something was wrong. There, in the salon, where stray sunbeams made patterns on the rich Damascus carpet and the light was still cool and dim and the air heavy with the scent of orange blossom and jasmine, part of her was crying out with pain and fear, and she knew which part it was. It had happened before, but never like this. Her twin had never suffered like this before.

But there was nothing she could do about it so she sat waiting, clasping her hands, and after a time she went to her mother in the kitchen and helped her chop parsley and pound wheat. Only when her mother had left the room for a moment did she hear a stealthy whisper, and turn, to see Huda beckoning to her through a crack in the door.

'Come,' breathed Huda, lifting a white scared face. 'Come quick! Amin says. Come and don't tell anybody. He's sitting under the orange trees, and, Lamia . . . shall I tell you what? . . . He's crying!'

Lamia ran. She found him, as Huda had said, sitting at the foot of an orange tree, his head in his hands. When he heard her coming, he looked up, his eyes dark with tragedy. His clothes reeked of gunpowder.

'Lamia,' he whispered, 'it has come . . . I must go . . . I think we shall all be needed . . . but our men were so cruel and violent. They needn't have done that . . .'

He shuddered and pressed his hands against his eyes as though to shut out some terrible sight.

'What did they do, Amin?' asked Lamia. But she too felt the horror and did not want to hear.

The boy's expression was haunted.

'We were attacked outside the church and our leader's bodyguard fell dead. I could not see . . . I was on the edge of a great crowd, and we all made for the river. There was

15

shouting and noise and very great anger. Then a bus came down the road toward the Camp ... Our militia lined up on either side of the road and shot ... I could see them through the smashed windows ... men, women and children ... screaming, dying, cut by glass ... they would not stop shooting ... Oh, Lamia, this is not war, this is murder, and now many will die ... I must go ...'

'Go where, Amin? You are all cold and shaking. Come in to Mother and rest.'

He shook his head violently. 'Not Mother!' he said. 'If I see Mother, I shall give in. Tell her ... you know what to tell her, Lamia. Come with me to Hanni's house.'

He was beginning to recover and to pull himself together, and she knew it was no use trying to stop him, so she followed him to the street at the side of the house. Already the news seemed to be spreading. People stood whispering in frightened groups and some were barricading their shop windows.

It was very quiet at Hanni's house, for Hanni's parents had gone to spend the day with their married daughter and Hanni, the youngest, was the only one at home. He came to the door in battle-dress, gun in hand, looking strangely old for his seventeen years. His face was grave but he seemed less shaken than Amin.

'Hurry up!' he said curtly. 'Headquarters will be expecting us by now. Your clothes are in there. Hurry up, and come.'

But, left alone with Lamia, his expression changed. She had never known him very well; he was just Amin's friend. But his face was suddenly gentle and he seemed to want to tell her something as he stood there awkwardly fingering his gun.

'You will fight?' she whispered.

He nodded. 'I think so; there are bound to be reprisals ... it was the act of madmen!' He gazed out of the window. His house stood on a hill and beyond the blossom in the garden the city sloped to the sea. Behind the great skyscrapers and hotels they could see the sparkle of the Mediterranean. 'It's worth fighting for,' he said simply. 'Why should we be driven out by strangers?'

Amin was back in a few moments in a battle-dress too big for him. His cheek was still as smooth as a child's, and he looked scared and awkward and all wrong, like someone dressed up.

'Goodbye, my sister,' he said bravely. He hesitated, and then went on. 'Do one thing for us; go up to the church and pray in front of that crucifix . . . and go now. If you delay it may be too late; and tell my mother I'm sorry.'

They left, marching self-consciously down the road, guns cocked, and she was glad that she had something to do. Blinded with tears, she groped her way back through the orange groves, avoiding the streets, and took the path that led through the terraced olive plantations to the church. Crouching at the foot of the carved figure with the out-stretched arms, she looked up into the pale, expressionless face and remembered her brother's question. 'Can a dead Christ help us? Can those fixed, nail-pierced hands hold back fighting and war?' Yet she murmured every prayer she knew and knelt before the Virgin and every Saint in the church. But they had all died so long ago and they looked so wooden. Chilled and discouraged she slipped out into the living springing world, and the slopes of red anemones in the grass comforted her, for this was the season of wild flowers and birdsong and blossom, and out there in the sunshine death seemed meaningless.

She wandered home slowly, picking flowers as she went, for she was in no hurry to break the news to her mother. Besides, she was thinking about Hanni and Amin; Amin, so young and scared yet steadfast, Hanni with his grave tender eyes. She was sure that there was something he had wanted to say, but it had not been said, and she thought that if he had said it, it would have been something very important. She knew too that if he died today it would never be said, to her eternal loss. And then she wondered why she was thinking of Hanni at all when Amin was in danger.

And then, just as she was stooping to pick a flower, the thunder began, not far away this time, but on the eastern side of the river, the roar of heavy machine guns and mortars had started up. She saw the blue of the April sky suddenly stained with black smoke, and ran terrified to the door of her home which faced the mountains. Her mother was standing at the gate looking wildly up and down with Huda clinging to her skirts.

'Lamia, my child, come in quickly. Where's your brother?'

Huddled together in the salon, the sound of battle slightly dulled by the thick walls of the house and the blocks of flats that backed their home, Lamia sobbed out her story. 'I couldn't stop him, Mother,' she pleaded. 'Don't say that it was all my fault!'

Her mother stroked her hair. 'No, you couldn't stop him,' she said quietly. 'He loves his land, and he is a brave lad. It is good to have such a son. May God have mercy on him and on your father.'

'Where is Father?'

'Down at the shop; he was afraid of looting and destruction. He'll come home all right. The radio is announcing the safe areas and he'll make his way round. Come, I am going to get something to eat. Our little ones are hungry.'

She smiled down at their scared faces, lightening the tension, and they followed her to the kitchen, jostling against her like frightened lambs. But the bombardment was getting louder and fiercer and the acrid smell of burning and high explosive came seeping into the house.

'We are safe here, I think,' said their mother calmly, 'unless a rocket falls on the roof and sets fire to the top storey, or unless the block behind us burns. But I feel sorry for those who live in the west of the suburb. Come Lamia, let us bake bread. If this goes on till nightfall, we may have to shelter some of them. Thank God we are well stocked with food.'

Lamia stood at the doorway, watching the swelling stream of people hurrying toward the mountain. They came like ants from the streets and up through the orange groves in a terrified, bewildered procession. Women carried babies in their arms and bundles on their backs. Men bore little children on their shoulders and pushed prams and barrows piled high with household goods. Most pitiful were the old, stumbling along half dragged, half supported by relatives, or pushed aside by those who could move more quickly.

'But where are they all going?' asked Huda.

'Who knows?' replied Lamia. 'Some may have relatives in the villages; I think some will sleep on the mountainside tonight.'

'The convents will take in some,' said her mother. 'And if any turn aside we will also offer them shelter for the night.'

They worked hard, preparing food as for a siege, but time passes slowly when each minute, separately counted, fails to register the return of a father or brother, and the noise of the bombardment was so loud that at times they could hardly hear themselves speak. Now the sun would be setting over the sea but the tender colours of twilight would be hidden by the black pall of death that brooded over the district, and, in any case, their mother would not allow them to go to the back of the house.

And still the heavy shelling continued and the solid old house trembled with the impact, and at dusk the visitors began to arrive from the lower part of the suburb. They had sat out the day in cellars and basements, having nowhere else to flee to, but they could not face those terrible hours ahead. In a slight lull they had fled to their neighbours in the more sheltered eastern quarter and Lamia thought that her mother must have seemed to them like an angel of mercy as she welcomed them courteously to her salon and set food before them.

Some could only weep and tremble, others had strange and terrible stories to tell. One couple had fled with their three little children from a blazing house and sat mourning the total destruction of all their goods. Another small family arrived, bruised and cut, their hair and clothes white with dust and plaster, for the ceiling had fallen in on them. Then one came, silent, numb, shocked beyond weeping, carrying a little blasted body in her arms. Some had scarcely made the journey, caught in the cross-fire between the camp and the hill to the north, to say nothing of those terrible hooded snipers who crouched on the roofs of the derelict buildings. There were bodies lying in the streets, and road-blocks at every exit. Yet more kept arriving.

Lamia doled out food and coffee and listened to the tales in silence. Rosa was laying out the dead child in her own bedroom and comforting the dazed mother, until the ice melted and she was able to weep. But Elias had not returned, and Lamia thought of those bodies lying in the rubble. Yet she knew that Amin was alive, for while part of her felt his fear and danger, no part of her had died.

The night wore on; the bereaved mother, drugged by shock and sorrow, slept deeply, one arm flung across the sheet that covered her dead baby. Rosa bound up cuts and bathed bruises and served more coffee, soothing and comforting, and the children fell into heavy slumber. But Lamia remained wide awake, listening, until the cocks began to crow up in the mountain and the roar of the past twelve hours seemed to sink to a low grumble, broken only by the sharp crack of the occasional bullet. Nearly everyone was dozing by this time, and she crept to the door unnoticed and slipped out into the dawn.

Oh, the sweetness of the dark mountain air after the fetid atmosphere of the windowless passage where she had spent the night! It would soon be light and the cypresses stood like black swords against the paling sky to the south. She stood breathing deeply, conscious that the garden breathed too, and the scent of flowers and dew overcame the stink of explosives, and the birdsong was clear and piercing, because the bombardment had, for the moment, ceased. Morning always came in the end if you waited long enough.

Perhaps it was the unusual silence that woke people. In any case, when she slipped back inside, everyone was moving, gathering up their bundles and sleeping children, murmuring their thanks as they shuffled, heavy-eyed, towards the door. Even fighters have to rest sometime and it was important to make the most of the lull, for who knew how long one might have, to sweep up the glass and debris, prepare for the next onslaught, tend the wounded and bury the dead? In a very short time all had gone, and while the younger children still slept, Rosa and Lamia flung open doors and windows, hoovered the carpets and washed the dirty crockery. They were hard at work when a step was heard outside, and the next instant Rosa had run into her husband's arms.

He held her for a moment, moved and surprised by this sudden display of emotion from his dutiful, dignified wife. Then he pushed her gently away from him and said, 'Are you all right? And where's the boy?'

But they could not answer that question and his face seemed to turn old and grey before their eyes. Perhaps he had already guessed, for he knew his son. You cannot curtain the dawn or quench the spring or extinguish the fire of patriotism in the heart of a boy. But he sat down at the table, buried his face in his hands and groaned; for he had crept home through the grey morning that seemed to steal in, shrouded and ashamed, on blackened buildings and streets that were empty except for mounds hastily covered, on looted shops and demolished homes. He had asked himself in bitterness of spirit, 'To what purpose is this waste?' and he had found no true answer.

3

For three days and nights the battle raged, with lulls in the early morning, and Rosa's solid home, tucked between the mountain and the tall apartment blocks on the west, became an open shelter for families of terrified squatters, many of whose own homes, in the forefront of the battle, were fast being demolished by fire or ammunition, and some would creep home at dawn to find all their possessions taken by looters. Elias spent most of his time at the shop guarding his livelihood, while Rosa and Lamia soothed the children, fed the hungry, comforted the bereaved and tended shrapnel wounds. They were glad to be busy because it helped to pass the empty aching hours. For Amin had not returned.

But on the morning of the third day there was an eerie calm, and various well-known voices on the radio urged their followers to withdraw from the streets. It was quiet in their district, for although in some quarters there were signs of rejoicing, in the eastern suburbs people were dazed with destruction and loss, and many of them slept exhausted in their ruins, or tried pitifully to bury their dead with decency and dignity. It seemed like a ghost town – a blackened scar on the side of the April mountain. Lamia sat on the step dozing in the sunshine, and wondered whether she was dreaming when she opened her eyes and found Amin standing in front of her.

She gave a little cry and would have fainted, but he jerked her upright and she realized that his need was greater than hers and pulled herself together. His battle dress was caked with mud, his face streaked and lined with dirt and grease, his hair matted with dried blood. As she looked into his eyes she saw that they were bloodshot and haunted with sights of which he would never speak. Nor would he ever again weep at death, because he had seen too much of it. Then his mother came running to him, and Sami and Huda woke at her loud rapturous cry, and they too flung themselves on him.

'Who won?' shouted Huda. 'Tell us who won!'

'Yes, who won?' echoed Sami. 'And did you shoot anyone with your gun?'

'We held our suburbs,' said Amin. 'Mother, I want to wash and eat and sleep. Mother, get me some food!'

Her heart soared at his petulant, little-boy voice and by the time he had washed and changed, she had a meal on the table. Sami was bursting with questions but suddenly Amin's patience seemed to snap. 'Mother,' he cried, 'send them away! I want to eat and go to sleep . . . You stay, Mother.'

She sat beside him stitching a gay little skirt for Huda and the steady movement of her hands calmed his jangled nerves and the peace of her bowed face restored his sanity. The memory of the screams of a lacerated child, the stench of bodies left to lie where they fell, grew less vivid. He thought he could sleep.

He slept and slept, all day and all night, and his mother and Lamia, and later, his father, sat beside him in turns in case he should wake and want something. Late next morning he woke, rested and relaxed, and almost his old gay self. Only Lamia knew that he had changed and they would never again be as one; for in three short, terrible days he had travelled ahead into manhood.

Schools re-opened and, apart from the persistent snipers on the rooftops, the precarious peace held. People came back from the hills to their damaged or ruined homes and resumed life as best they could. Yet every day there were rumours of fresh clashes in the north, and such tales of murder, robbery and violence from the southern rim of the city that few would travel on the great highways. There was tension in the air, a restless feeling that the shelling and destruction had achieved nothing, that hatred still simmered and would soon boil over. Hanni and Amin spent much time together, sitting on the house steps, talking, and at night they would disappear, no one knew where. And sometimes Kamal would stroll up from the camp beyond the orange groves and on these occasions Lamia noticed that Hanni always fell silent. One night when Kamal had gone, Hanni said, very seriously, 'Why do you allow that boy to come here? Did he not fight for his side, as we fought for ours?'

'But the truce is signed,' said Amin. 'And he has always been my good school-friend. Should I turn against him in time of peace because fate has placed us on different sides? Besides, we do not know whether he knows that we fought.'

'Friend he may have been,' replied Hanni, 'but if war breaks out again he'll once more be your enemy. For your own safety and for his, let him stay in his own place. I don't trust him.'

Lamia glanced at her brother and saw the stubborn look that she knew so well come into his face, and loved him for it. Amin was loyal and he would not give up because others doubted. Kamal might not come to the house again but the friendship would continue; and three days later the matter was put to the test. Their father had gone to Damascus on business when the invitation arrived to Kamal's birthday party, so there was nothing to stop Amin accepting.

'You'll come too, Lamia,' he announced. 'Each of us boys can take a girl friend and you, at the moment, are my best girl friend. As this may not always be the case, you had better make the best of it while you can.'

Lamia laughed. All the girls liked Amin but so far, taken up with his cause, he had had little time for such matters. But when summer came they would go to the beach together and she would introduce him to her friends. She was disappointed that Hanni would not come to the party although pressed to do so. He stood at his door watching them as they set out.

'I think you are a fool to go,' said Hanni quietly, 'and a bigger fool to take your sister.'

Amin laughed but his eyes were angry.

'Are you afraid, Hanni?' he demanded. 'And why must you always be so suspicious? Are there no laws of hospitality? And what could they do to us at a birthday party, anyhow?'

'No, I'm not afraid,' replied Hanni, still unruffled; 'but I'm sensible, and in any case, my father has forbidden me, and so would yours if he were here. Does your mother know where you are going?'

Amin looked uncomfortable. He had not told his mother where he was going, only that he was taking Lamia to a school party and she had been glad to see them go together, for she sensed Lamia's sadness. She had ironed her daughter's scarlet dress with loving care, and as she watched them leave the house she wondered for the hundredth time how she, a simple village girl, had managed to produce such a merry handsome son and such a glowing daughter.

'I will not have it said that I do not trust my friend,' replied Amin haughtily. 'However, it's your loss, not mine. We'll tell you about it this evening.'

Hanni shrugged his shoulders and looked at Lamia; the scarlet dress suited her dark beauty and her hair was brushed to show the gleam of her gold earrings. Her eyes were bright with happiness for just at that moment there

26

was no gulf between her and Amin. In their pleasures they were still one.

'Well, look after her,' said Hanni softly, and Lamia felt sorry that he disapproved. She turned her head and smiled shyly at him and he smiled back before they both disappeared into the shade of the orange groves. It was quiet and cool under the deep foliage and they were close in spirit as of old. For the first time, Amin talked of his experiences as though Lamia knew all about how scared he had been and how passionately he had longed to live. 'They nearly got me,' he said wistfully. 'The shrapnel grazed my head ... and now life seems so beautiful, and there's so much to see and do; but I think many of us young ones will die before it's over. Lamia, did you go up to the church as I told you to?'

'Yes; but I didn't stay long. Those images seem so wooden and dead. Can they really help, Amin?'

He laughed.

'Those images aren't God. Somewhere there must be a God who is alive ... a Creator ... Someone who controls the stars and the sea and makes things grow.

'There's something else I keep wondering about; if I'd been shot, would that have been the end, or is there somewhere else? I wish I knew.'

'Mother thinks there is.'

'Mother's not our generation and she hasn't had our education. She accepts all the priest tells her and asks no questions. I never really thought much about it before but when you hear the bullets whizzing past, it's different ... I suddenly found myself crying out to Someone who seemed to be there. I wanted to live but if I had to die I wanted to be ready. What I really feared was just to be nothing, and cease to exist.'

They were nearing the house now and they could hear

27

the loud blaring of a discotheque. They walked slowly, prolonging the pleasure of just being together.

'When all this is over,' said Amin suddenly, 'and our country unthreatened and our heritage restored, I'm going to find out about these things; and if I go into battle again, don't forget, whatever you think about it, to go to the church and pray in front of the crucifix. You never know . . .'

The party was already in full swing and Kamal saw them and came out to meet them. He seemed rather constrained and took little notice of Lamia.

'Where's Hanni?' he asked abruptly.

'Not coming,' replied Amin, shaking his hand. 'A blessing on your birthday.'

As they entered the room, Amin looked round surprised. He had understood that the whole class was coming, but he and Lamia seemed to be the only ones from their suburb, or belonging to their particular political party. Had all the others been afraid? However, there was nothing to be done about it now, and they might as well enjoy themselves. He was soon stuffing himself with the delicious food and jitterbugging as gaily as anyone. They would leave before sunset, he decided, and get home in the light.

And then suddenly it happened. Lamia, with a spoonful of ice-cream half way to her mouth, noticed the sudden dead silence and looked up. 'It can't be true,' she thought. But it was.

Two hooded gunmen stood in the doorway and an armoured car was drawn up at the steps. Rifles cocked, they barked their orders. 'Girls to one side! Boys, over to the other!'

Everyone obeyed instantly; one girl fainted and another began crying hysterically, but the muzzle of a gun pointed at her, silenced her immediately.

'Boys! Moslems over there, Christians stand still.'

The group moved to the left, leaving Amin standing alone dazed and ashen-faced. The gunmen turned to Kamal. 'Where is the other?' he demanded.

Kamal, who had affected indignant surprise, turned crimson under his tan. 'He did not come,' he muttered.

'Right, we'll have this one.' And Amin was marched at gun-point to the car. But at the door he suddenly turned, and his eyes, huge and desperate, were fixed on his twin. 'I'm sorry, Lamia,' he said steadily; 'tell our father . . .', but he was prodded into the car with the butt of a rifle, and Elias was never to know what message his son had sent him.

No one stopped Lamia as she rushed to the steps, and he turned again, leaning forward, and gave her a brave, pitiful little smile. Then, with a violent acceleration, the vehicle roared off in the direction of the camps.

4

Two days passed in a frenzy of phoning, visits to Government departments, and Security Forces, but all to no avail. Amin was, after all, just one insignificant victim of the wave of kidnapping, murder and worse that had broken out since the outburst of fighting. Law and order had collapsed and the temporary Government was tottering. In spite of the uneasy, technical 'peace', armed clashes, bomb explosions, and other incidents of terror and violence were the order of the day in the north of the city, and one lost boy attracted little attention. Besides, he was only sixteen and had no legal right to be involved with the militia.

Lamia hardly remembered returning home; someone had driven her in a car, but she could not remember who. She had been quite hysterical, and only the pressure of her mother's hand on her forehead and the sound of her mother's quiet weeping, had restored the girl to some sort of sanity. She had lain awake nearly all night and the darkness had seemed hot and heavy with her grief, her fear, and her hate, but mostly with her hate. For Kamal had betrayed his friend; he had known that Amin had been fighting for his side, and had deliberately enticed him to a place where he could be abducted, and Lamia's hatred was so strong, that if her father had not hidden Amin's gun, she would have picked it up and started off to avenge her brother. So the hours passed in frenzied activity on her father's side and in quiet weeping and waiting on her mother's side, and Lamia waited too, shut up in her private hell. For hating is a lonely business and it cut her off from her mother. Rosa grieved and spent hours in front of the crucifix, but perhaps she loved too deeply to have any room for hate.

Lamia climbed to the church several times and muttered prayers in front of every image and statue. Her brother had told her to do so, and besides, it passed the time. But the Christ on the cross had been overcome by death, and there seemed no message of hope in his dead face; she wondered dully what Amin's face would look like if they shot him, and he seemed to have no part at all in this musty old building. Only on the way back, as she passed through the vineyards and saw the young vine leaves unfolding and the small tendrils reaching up and clutching to climb, could she picture him again: the brightness of his eyes, the aliveness of his young face, the growing, questing spirit reaching up to light and truth. She remembered their last walk. 'I wish I knew ... I'm going to find out ...' He had said those words just before the house came in sight, and when she thought about the house, black hatred engulfed her and shut out every other memory.

She fell asleep by the open window that night, deeply conscious of his loneliness and fear but too worn out to vigil with him any longer. For the first time since his disappearance she slept soundly and woke suddenly, strong and refreshed, but quite unable to remember what had happened to them. It was still dark although the sky over the rim of the mountain was paling, and the great morning star hung low. She was conscious of some tragedy hanging over them all, but that part of her that had grieved and feared seemed to have died. The dawn wind, rustling her curtain, breathed of joy unspeakable and the music of joy was all about her: the twittering of waking birds, and the laughter of children who run out into an early summer morning, laughing riotously at nothing at all, just because they are happy and together; she and Amin had so often laughed like that. Then it all gradually came back to her and she wondered how she could ever have thought of joy, and what on earth could Amin be laughing about now? She turned over, wept into her pillow and slept again.

She was still asleep some hours later when a young man came to the door and asked, rather awkwardly, for Elias. The body of a boy had been dumped just inside the orange groves, and, as Elias had a son missing, would he please go and investigate?

Elias walked to the place and knelt beside the body of his son. They must have held him for questioning for he had not been dead long. He lay as though asleep in his soiled party clothes and there was no look of horror on his face. Elias examined him swiftly and a great rush of thankfulness swept over him and then receded before the tide of his grief. For Amin had been killed by one clean bullet shot through his head and he had not been tortured or mutilated. In this, at least, God had been merciful.

There was nothing to be done about it except to fetch help and carry him home to his mother; to wash him and robe him and lay him in state before bearing him to the grave, and to start the traditional days of mourning. Hearts might break but the conventions must be kept and the necessary work must be done, and this was a good thing for these conventions were like stakes to which you clung in the flood lest you be carried away and drowned. But this time there was not even the comfort of the great mourning due to the death of an eldest son, for death threatened everywhere on the roads and people were afraid to travel. Even the neighbours feared to be in the streets after dark, and besides . . . so many eldest sons had died.

But Hanni came and sat dumb and stricken beside the body of his friend, and Lamia saw the anguish in his eyes. It was the first time she had seen him since the party, although he had been feverishly carrying messages and making enquiries. To begin with she had not wanted to see him, for Amin had died and he had lived; but he too had been very near to death and, watching his misery, she was suddenly glad that he was alive. For he was a boy and could wield a gun and through him she might now achieve the great driving purpose of her life at that moment – to avenge her brother's murder.

They carried Amin to his grave in the mellow light of that early May evening, up through the sprouting vineyards and ripening orchards to the cemetery on the hillside. The men followed, but the black-robed women stayed in the house. One by one the visitors left to get home before sunset, and by twilight only a few of the nearest kinsmen and neighbours remained in that empty, empty room. Little Huda snuggled into her mother's lap, and Rosa rocked her like a baby, singing the songs that little children have sung for centuries past, but there was no one to comfort Lamia. She sat at the window staring at the darkening hillside. The men would soon be coming home and Amin would be left alone.

They came, walking slowly, and she watched them taking leave of each other and going off with bowed heads, each to his own home. But Hanni and her father stood at the gate for a long time, talking, for he had only a few hundred yards to go. She stood waiting behind a jasmine bush, for she wanted to speak to him, and when her father passed her, unnoticing, she slipped out of the gate and ran down the road.

'Hanni!'

He turned and waited for her. His face was dark against the sunset, but hers was very bright. The light burned in her eyes and there was a scarlet spot on each of her cheeks. He was too wretched to register just then, but later on he remembered that she had looked very beautiful.

'Lamia,' he cried, 'Oh Lamia! I almost wish I had gone and died with him!'

'What use would that have been? Hanni, I want you to promise to do something for me.'

'Anything I can, I'll do.'

'Hanni, you must avenge my brother's death, and you must do it soon. I cannot rest while that traitor still lives.'

'But Lamia, how can we be sure who the traitor was? There were many there from the camp.'

She tossed back her hair impatiently.

'Of course we know,' she said. 'It was Kamal; he pretended to be surprised, but I heard what they said. "Where's the other one?" they asked him, and he answered "He didn't come." They wanted you too, Hanni. You were both betrayed; you must go with your gun and shoot him.'

'And if they were asking for me, they are waiting for me in the orange groves. If I took that path I should be dead before I ever reached the house. God will avenge, Lamia, and if ever I meet him in battle I will do my part.'

She looked at him scornfully.

'Are you afraid, Hanni?' she asked rather bitterly. 'I should have thought you would have been in more of a hurry than to leave it to chance. After all, he was your friend as well as my brother.'

She wished she could see his shadowed face, but his voice, when he spoke, was hard and forced, almost as though he was pushing out his thoughts very slowly, from some hidden depth of anguish.

'I'm not afraid of dying, Lamia, if that's what you mean . . . in fact, I would gladly commit suicide at the moment if my death helped anyone . . . but what's the point of it all? If I'm afraid of anything, it's the thought of my parents weeping beside the body of their only son, weeping as

yours and many others are doing . . . and to what purpose?
. . . who is the richer for it?'

He kicked a stone savagely down the hill.

'I gathered you thought there was some point in defending your heritage, your faith, and your country — but perhaps not!' the girl spoke sarcastically and Hanni flared up.

'What are we doing to our country, except destroying it? . . . Is this war? What we do is revenge, not defence . . . They kill some soldiers in the north and we blow up a woman and her children in the suburbs, and they snipe an only son to exact payment. Where will it end? When will it ever stop? Many, many will die before it's all over. Oh Lamia, I wish you could go right away and be safe!'

She started as his tone changed suddenly from anger to passionate despair. She longed to fling herself against him and weep and weep. But he did not share her fierce hatred and thirst for revenge and she turned away coldly.

'I would not wish to go, Hanni, when my country is in such danger. Perhaps before long they will allow girls to fight and then I shall do what you do not seem to wish to do.'

She ran up the hill and in at her front gate. Her father sat slumped on the verandah staring out toward the mountain, and he did not notice her. Inside it was quiet and nearly dark. Soon they would switch on the light and prepare food for their few remaining guests, but for the moment the mourners sat listlessly and the children had fallen asleep. Her mother had gone into the bedroom and knelt in front of the crucifix with a lighted candle in her hand.

'Mother,' whispered Lamia through her teeth, 'Where is Amin?'

Her mother turned and her profile was like carved

ivory; like a statue in the church, thought Lamia. The girl crouched on the floor and Rosa drew her close and was silent for a long time. When at last she spoke her voice was troubled.

'Amin was a good boy,' she said. 'I do not think he will need to do much purgatory. I shall pray and light candles for him . . .'

Lamia shuddered; she had not really thought about purgatory. Amin was her twin, her shared life, and no part of her today had been conscious of his suffering. Perhaps she had been too wrapped up in her own grief or perhaps death severed the bond. Anyhow, she thought, I shall never know, so what is the good of thinking about it? To her mother she replied, 'I went to the church and prayed too; he told me to. But it didn't do any good, did it?'

'He told you to? Then he was a believer?'

Had Lamia looked up, she would have seen the marble statue illumined, but her face was hidden in her mother's dress.

'He said he didn't know; it might do some good. He said that later on he was going to find out . . . but it didn't do any good, did it. Mother, what's the use of it all? What's the use of anything? . . . that little wooden dead Christ . . . it couldn't save him, could it?'

There was another long silence and then her mother spoke again:

'My daughter, I was a village girl, and village girls did not ask questions as you do now. My husband is not a religious man, and the priest does not tell me much. There must be so much more to know that I do not know, and you will read and travel and find out. But I do know that Christ died because he loved us and it's that love that I remember.'

'But what's the use of loving, if he can't save? Mother, what *is* the point of it all?'

Hanni's words had impressed her more deeply than she knew. Yet sitting there with her mother's hand stroking her hair she recognised part of the answer to her own question. For love can be very comforting even if it cannot save.

5

The days dragged and the weather was getting hot. Lamia's bedroom faced west and she woke each morning to see the heat haze rising from the river. It cleared as the sun rose above the eastern peaks, streaming across the rooftops, and the great curve of the coast southward sparkled silver. The wild flowers were beginning to fade but roses and syringa still blossomed in the garden under her window; but her heart was too heavy to notice the scent and light and colour any more, and she would go down to breakfast heavy-eyed and listless.

The children had stopped going to school, for the roads into the city were too dangerous. There was no actual war, and people struggled to return to normal; only continual sniping and looting and terrible cases of individual brutality. Lamia, in any case, could not return to school, for local mourners continued to visit and her mother insisted on keeping to the traditional ways. She sat and received condolences, served coffee and engaged in small talk; the hours seemed endless and she hated every moment of it.

She leaned on her window-sill one morning, staring moodily into space, when she heard a whistle and, looking down, she saw Hanni standing by the rose-bush in his battle-dress waiting for her. Her heart beat a little quicker and she glanced in the mirror for though she scorned his attitude, she had longed to see him again. She ran downstairs with a lighter step than usual, and came to him across the grass. Her pale face and black dress looked strangely out of place in that sparkling summer garden and a great protective tenderness rose up in Hanni's heart; but he spoke abruptly.

'Lamia, have you listened to the radio this morning?'

'Yes; this Government is packing up. Who'll be next, do you think?'

'I don't know who'll be next, but I know *what* will be next: bitter fighting. They've sent a message to all those in the party bidding them to be ready. When they summon us, I shall go. I . . . I . . . I just came to say goodbye.'

'Well, you're not going yet. Where will you fight?'

'I don't know; to the south, I should imagine, round the camps. Lamia, if I see him, I'll repay . . . unless he gets me first.'

His expression was grim and uncertain. With Lamia standing there against the rose-bush, he wanted desperately to live. But even as they stood talking, the familiar rumble, as of distant thunder, reached them across the rooftops.

'Where is it now?' asked Lamia.

'Near the port,' he replied.

The sound seemed to quench all other communication. Beside the voice of the guns all the things they had wanted to say, all the things that had seemed so important, seemed banal and pointless. They stared at each other bleakly and an awkward silence fell between them.

'Well, I'd better be going,' said Hanni at last.

'Yes, and I'd better go into breakfast,' said Lamia.

'If I go, I'll try and see you again.'

'You may not have time, so goodbye.'

'Goodbye; take care of yourself.'

'Same to you.'

Once again the roar of the guns; a small wind breathed in the rose bush and a crimson rosebud trembled just above Lamia's head. Hanni picked it and handed it to her.

'A token of life,' he said. 'I'll come back, Lamia.'

'With your vow fulfilled,' she added, and saw the light

die out of his eyes because she would not show whether she cared about his return or not. He turned away and left her fingering the rose.

He did not see her again before he went into action. The call came suddenly, early in the morning, and if he came and stood under her window in the half-light, breathing her name very softly lest, by any chance, she might be awake, she knew nothing about it. She only heard that he had gone, later in the day when the great bombardment had started and the people were once again fleeing from the lower part of the suburb, when the stink of explosives tainted the air and the thunder of mortar bombs rocked the district. Elias was still in the city and Rosa and Lamia started on a frenzy of baking, and opened their door to the guests who soon started arriving.

It seemed as though all parties were taking advantage of the delay in forming a new Government to move into the streets and terrorize with sniping and bombs and heavy artillery. Down in the camp they fired rockets unceasingly from an abandoned building, and the high apartment blocks that sheltered Lamia's house received two direct hits. The electricity was cut and when night fell they lit candles. The soft glow shone on the dazed, sometimes bruised faces, and looking round, Lamia suddenly noticed that Sami was missing.

She said nothing to her mother who was in the kitchen; he could not be far. She ran into the garden calling his name but there was no answer. She looked up into the sky, terrible and aflame behind the buildings and immediately she knew where he was. She raced to the roof and found him standing by the parapet, arms folded, legs apart, outlined against the glow.

'Sami,' she yelled, 'come back at once! Anything may fall there.'

He took no notice, and struggled fiercely when she

seized hold of his collar and dragged him to a more sheltered position. 'Are you mad, Sami?' she asked sharply. 'D'you want us to lose our second boy?'

He grinned up at her. 'D'you know what, Lamia?' he replied.

'What, you crazy boy!'

'The bombs are falling at the bottom of the orange groves. There's a great fire burning. I think Kamal's house is burning, and perhaps Kamal is burning. Don't you hope he is? . . . oh, Lamia, I wish I was old enough! I wish I had a gun!'

She looked down at him with approval, for his mood was nearer to hers than anyone else's. He was small and thin and eager and she had never taken him too seriously before, but now he seemed like a true comrade. Together they crouched in a sheltered part of the roof, looked toward the spot where the fire raged, and hated and felt good.

They all slept fitfully in the passages with the families they were beginning to know quite well, and once again Lamia woke early because of the strange, unwonted silence as the bombardment died down for a few hours. Once again, she felt stifled and longed for air, and once again she slipped out into the summer morning. She never knew why she took the path into the orange groves, the same path which she and Amin had trodden so gaily on their last walk together, and she followed it a little way down into the trees. It was a foolhardy thing to do, for it led straight into the region of the camp, and she did not mean to go far. She was well inside her own Christian suburb, safely enclosed in the deep green foliage and pungent smell of the orange trees in flower, but her feet seemed to be carrying her on until, on turning a corner, she stopped and caught her breath in horror. Just a few yards ahead of her, something was lying in the path.

She knew what it was at once and her first instinct was

to scream and run. But then she remembered that Amin had been found lying in the orange groves and she felt a consuming desire to see what sort of person this was. She crossed herself, summoned up all her courage, stepped forward and looked.

A woman in the clothing of a Palestinian refugee lay face downward. She had probably fled, wounded, from a burning house and, not knowing where to run by night, she had staggered into enemy territory and fallen under the trees. There was a shrapnel wound in her head and her clothing was blood-stained. She was quite dead, and Lamia felt no pity for her, for she was one of the race that had killed her brother.

Or was she quite dead? Lamia's heart gave a lurch of fear, for the cloak that covered the body on the grass suddenly quivered. Rooted to the spot she watched, unable to move a muscle, while the folds of the cloak rose and fell as though a struggle was going on underneath. Then the border was pushed back, and Lamia found herself gazing into two dark eyes, bright with sleep, set in a dirty brown face. They peered at her from beneath a tangle of black curls, puzzled but not afraid.

'Mama,' said the child, and the corners of its mouth turned down.

It struggled out and crouched beside the still figure calling it with baby words and giving it little pushes and jerks. Finding no response, the child lay down beside it, snuggling as close as it could, and began to suck two fingers; and Lamia stood watching, hardly daring to breathe.

She could not leave it there. A baby was a baby, whatever its race, and her mother would know what to do with it. It looked about two years old and she had no idea whether it was a girl or a boy. Pulling herself together, she stooped and took the child in her arms, and although it whimpered at first and looked back at its mother, it soon stuck its fingers into its mouth again and laid its head on Lamia's shoulder. After all, the ground had been prickly and these arms were soft and warm. Besides, it was hungry, and this person seemed to be going somewhere. So she climbed slowly back up the path between the trees with her gift in her arms. The child was dirty, grimed with smoke, and smelling, among other things, of high explosive, but from the moment it had looked up trustfully into her eyes Lamia had started to love it and she knew she would fight as fiercely to keep it as she would to get her revenge.

'Moomi wants a drink,' said the child suddenly.

'You shall have a drink, Moomi,' said Lamia, holding it close. They had reached the garden gate by now and the morning was still quite quiet. The guests were gone. Huda sat on the doorstep eating her breakfast and Sami was still asleep.

'What's that, sister?' asked Huda, looking up at the bundle.

'A baby, Huda. It's coming to live with us.'

'God be praised! I like babies. Let me look at it, Lamia. Is it a boy or a girl?'

'I don't know yet, but it doesn't matter. It wants a drink first. Fetch me some milk and some yoghurt and I'll feed it here on the step, and then I'm going to find some clean clothes and give it a bath. Fetch Mother, Huda. She'll know where to find everything.'

It was a little boy, well-fed and healthy; beautiful in every way except for a great purple birthmark on his back. He called himself Moomi, probably short for Abdel Moomin. Rosa still had some of Huda's baby clothes laid away in a chest, in lavender and bay leaves; she brought them out gladly, for the listless look had gone from Lamia's face and Huda was laughing for the first time since her brother died. 'It is surely a gift from the Blessed Mother,' thought Rosa, for though she felt sure that her own broken heart would never heal, the child would certainly bring some comfort to her daughters. And when fed, washed, and clothed in clean garments he sat proudly on Lamia's lap while she wrestled with the tangles in his curls, everyone gathered round him and agreed that he was a most winning little lad.

Everything charmed him; he trotted round the garden, entranced with the flowers, until the rumble and thunder of a new bombardment drove them all indoors. But Huda brought him a bunch of roses and he sat on the floor in a patch of sunlight, playing with the petals, and talking all the time in a baby language they could not understand. He explored everywhere, but Lamia seemed to have taken the place of the poor huddled figure in the orange grove, for he kept glancing round to make sure she was still there. If she went into the next room, he became worried and would follow her and try to pull her back by her skirt. And the day did not seem quite so long to anyone, except to Rosa, whose husband had not yet come home.

About five o'clock Moomi began to look pensive, so Lamia gave him a drink of milk, undressed him and clothed him in a little white nightgown, rather too big for him. He was already fast asleep, completely inured to the roar of the bombardment, yet he seemed restless. When Lamia laid him in the bed she had improvised for him, he sat up again.

'Ba,' he said in a puzzled voice; 'ah, Ba!'

'Ba's not here now,' said Lamia, laying her cheek against his. 'Lie down now, my loved one. I'm here.'

He lay down obediently, sucking his fingers, but his face wore a sad, faraway look. As Lamia sat watching him, he gave a deep sigh and fell asleep, and a few minutes later a horn hooted in the yard, and Rosa rushed to welcome her husband. He looked grey and drained and she ran to heat coffee, while the children gathered round; but he motioned them away. 'Let me talk with your mother first,' he said. 'Is everything all right?'

Lamia and the younger ones went into the kitchen to prepare the evening meal and Rosa sat with her husband. 'How late you are,' she said; 'and how much I feared for you. Stay here with us, my husband. How much rather would I lose the money than lose you.'

'Then how shall we live, foolish woman? I have left Michel with a gun to guard the shop at present. It is still some distance from the fighting but the looting is terrible. I have seen them walk into undefended shops and walk out with carpets and yards of material over their arms, and everywhere sniping and atrocities. The radio was announcing the safe streets and I came home on the eastern road . . . a car came past . . . a body was hooked to the number plate . . . dragged through the streets . . . women stood on the pavement laughing . . .'

She shuddered. 'They are like devils from hell,' she said.

He glanced at her. 'They were our people,' he said after a moment, 'they had hung a crucifix on the car. The church is behind us; the brothers themselves are coming from the monasteries and pitching into the fighting with their kalashnikov rifles. We must hold our place in this new Government . . . but today it was as though all sides were behaving like devils from hell. Whose is that baby?'

Rosa hesitated and looked round for her children. They were standing in the doorway and she beckoned them forward for she felt sure she was going to need a lot of support.

'Lamia found him,' she said. 'His mother had been shot. I think she had run up through the groves, and come too far in her fear; she had died of shrapnel wounds.'

'Then the child is a Palestinian.'

'Well, yes . . . but a child is a child, Elias. Our girls were happy playing with it today.'

'Very well, let it sleep here tonight, and tomorrow I will leave it with the nuns at the convent on my way to work.'

There was a sudden uproar. Huda burst into loud crying and Lamia stood in front of her father, cheeks burning, hands clasped.

'Father, I want to keep him!'

His eyes flashed.

'The child of our enemies, and your brother not three weeks dead. I tell you, I will not have this brat in our house.'

'Father, we have lost one brother; let us keep this one.'

His taut nerves gave way and his anger blazed out.

'So! this little bastard can take the place of our brother, can it? You have forgotten him already . . . be silent, you fool of a girl, or I'll throw him out now, this minute!'

The hubbub was terrible; Huda roared and Lamia cried hysterically. Sami stamped his foot and Rosa wrung her hands. Elias continued to bellow above the uproar and a tremendous rattle of machine guns broke out not far from the house. They had kept their backs to the innocent cause of all the disturbance and nobody noticed when he sat up in bed and rubbed his eyes. He could sleep through any bombardment but he was not used to this sort of noise, and there was something familiar and splendid about it, something he had been missing. He had lost his mother, but he had found other safe arms and kind faces, and as much food as he wanted. But his father had gone off with the Commandos two days previously and no one had taken his place. The sound of an angry masculine voice denouncing something or other was sweet and familiar. Moomi climbed out of bed and floated, like a small lost angel, into the circle of candle-light. His eyes were bright and vague with half-forgotten dreams and his nightgown trailed behind him. He went straight to Elias and put two starfish hands on his knees.

'Ba!' said Moomi joyfully. 'Ah, Ba!'

There was sudden dead silence in the room; Huda stopped as though turned off at the main; and Lamia held her breath.

Moomi was holding up his arms and Elias lifted him into his lap like one mesmerized. The child snuggled against him, warm, fragrant and very sleepy. But before he closed his eyes he gave a drowsy chuckle, put up one hand and pulled Elias's beard. And suddenly Elias began to laugh; he laughed till the tears ran down his cheeks and all the others joined in. When the frightened people began knocking on the door at sunset asking for shelter for the night, they found the family still laughing, and Elias sat in the middle of the group nursing a curly enemy baby, who slept clutching the lapel of his coat.

6

No one ever mentioned the idea of Moomi leaving again, although Elias had a notice put in the local paper and informed the nuns, in case enquiries were made. But to everyone's relief, there was no reply, and within a matter of days he was completely accepted as one of the family, and Elias found himself waiting eagerly, when he opened the door, for the patter of small feet and the ecstatic cry of 'Ba! Ah, Ba!' There was some talk of a sensible Christian name, but Moomi somehow suited him, and Moomi he remained.

Fighting continued on and off, in spite of Cabinets forming, crumbling and reforming, and for a time people feared to walk in the streets because of the relentless snipers on the rooftops. No one was safe; people died in their armchairs, in the bath, sitting at their tables, and others simply disappeared. Yet as the weather grew really hot the latest frail summer truce seemed to hold, and there were no immediate, massive bombardments. The city dwellers began to lift up their heads and repair their burned, shelled homes, and to venture out into the street. They even went to the beach and swam, their guns laid alongside their picnic baskets. 'There will be no fourth round,' they said to each other, 'Praise be to God, it is over.'

Elias took Sami and Huda to the beach but Lamia stayed at home with her mother who was still officially in mourning, and dressed in deep black. All the glow and vitality seemed to have drained from the girl's life as though some part of her had truly died, and she seemed interested in nothing except her studies and Moomi. She had missed so much school and no examinations had been held, so she would sit on the verandah under the shade of the great vine, poring over her books, while Moomi sat with his toys on the floor, chattering away and quite unconcerned as to whether anyone was listening or not. He was a beautiful child, who showed every sign of having been loved and well cared for since birth; his dimples and great black eyes were made for laughter, and even Rosa's sad face brightened when he appeared.

In these sweltering days of deep depression, he was Lamia's lifeline. Without him, she would have woken each morning to wonder why she should go on existing but he was usually awake first, jumping up and down in his cot, shouting joyfully for attention. People might suffer and die and disappear, but Moomi still had to be bathed and fed. His small eager feet led her on from hour to hour, and when ministering to him, she could forget. She looked after him almost entirely, fighting off her jealousy when he toddled off to play with Huda, or climbed on to her mother's lap, and Rosa, watching, and yearning over her daughter, wondered rather vaguely whether the Christ Child had come amongst them to comfort them. But Moomi was not at all her idea of the Christ Child. He was far too merry.

Lamia saw very little of Hanni. He had come back from the last onslaught with a shrapnel wound on his face, and he had told her that the area round Kamal's home was mostly destroyed; but he had not shared her fierce passion for revenge and she felt out of tune with him. In any case, he had got a holiday job as an orderly in one of the biggest hospitals in the city, and he seldom came home. The road from the western to the eastern part of the city was too dangerous to travel often.

But one Saturday she took Huda and Moomi for a little walk up the mountain, and he saw her from his window and came after her. They sat on the wall while the children joined the first grape-pickers and stuffed themselves with fruit. The shimmering heat had subsided and the last golden light lay over the terraced vineyards, the ravaged city and the line of sea where the sun dipped to the horizon. Neither could think of anything to say to each other, and Lamia remembered the day when they had stood waiting for Amin to put on his battle dress, and there had been something to say, but it had not been said. It still had not been said, and probably never would be, she thought drearily, but the silence was getting oppressive so she asked him whether he thought there would be any more fighting.

His face fell; he had not wanted to talk about fighting.

'Of course,' he replied, 'nobody's got what they want. Everybody lost; nobody won.'

'Well, perhaps they'll just let it be.'

'Not they; everyone is thirsting for revenge. The young men are training in hide-outs all over the mountain. It just needs a spark and the whole country will be set ablaze.'

'Are you training?'

He hesitated; he knew that, deep down, she despised him.

'If war breaks out again on a big scale, I suppose I shall fight like the rest, but at present I am busy in the hospital. Who is that child, Lamia? I've seen him with you before.'

She reddened. 'His mother was killed,' she replied abruptly. 'I found him beside her dead body in the orange groves, so I brought him home.'

'In the groves? Then what nationality was his mother?'

'Well . . . she had come up from the camp.'

Hanni laughed. 'Your bark is worse than your bite, Lamia,' he said, 'and I don't wonder.' For Moomi had come trotting up through the vineyards, his cheeks and lips stained purple, and was holding up his arms. Hanni watched the girl's sealed young face soften into tenderness as she lifted the child on to her lap and kissed his hair. He smiled, and sighed, and went home.

Lamia called Huda. She wished that Hanni had waited. The sunset over the sea was crimson now; the colour of blood, she thought with a shudder. It would pale into grey twilight before they got home, like dead young faces drained of life and light. Hanni's words had depressed her deeply and her heart ached; if only he had waited! Any day now the holocaust might come and he might die, and there would be grey silence between them for ever; for nothing had been said.

It came when the harvests were ended and the vine leaves turning crimson on the terraces. It was not unexpected; tales of horror and massacre had been pouring in from the north and from the mountains like black streams that threatened to flood the capital. Fighting and looting broke out as never before and if it had not been for the voice of the radio persistently guiding people away from the dangerous streets and into the safe areas, Elias would never have got to and fro. He and his assistant slept at the shop now with their guns beside them, for although they were not yet in the battle zone, looters had little respect for the curfew. He would make his way home by roundabout routes in the early mornings, and arrive home grey with fatigue, to pour out fresh tales of horror to Rosa as he ate his breakfast. On one September morning his face looked ashen as he climbed the steps. He ate in silence, and his family knew what had happened, for the radio had already announced it; the bombing of an area not very far from his shop had resulted in the collapse of a hotel. All the inmates, mostly foreigners, were buried in the rubble and nothing could be done to save them.

Rosa implored him not to return. 'We have enough to live on,' she pleaded. 'Bring your goods and store them at home.'

He shook his head. 'I should need a van,' he said, 'and besides, they would commandeer my car at the checkpoints if they saw all that stuff. The shop is not in the direct firing line — at least, not yet. The battle is further to the west and in the southern suburbs. People still buy, but so many shops have been emptied and looted, and the looters are no longer ashamed. They drive up in cars and walk out openly with armfuls of expensive goods. Sometimes you cannot help laughing. I saw a man drive up in a Mercedes and park it outside a bombed cigarette factory. He came out laden with piles of boxes, only to find that someone had driven off in his car. There are strange stories abroad, Rosa. I have even seen armoured lorries with masked, armed girls going into battle.'

Lamia pricked up her ears. Perhaps life might be worthwhile after all. Amin had died for his country. 'Ready for your call, my Lebanon,' they had sung at school and her heart had thrilled with patriotism. She thought about it as she strapped Moomi into his pushchair and went down to the village to stand in the bread queue. Sami and Huda were back at the local school, but her school was in the city and had not been able to re-open. The daily queueing for food had become a way of life now, buying from traders who collected their produce from farmers on the outskirts, and trundled it in on barrows. Of course prices had soared and the good things they had so lavishly enjoyed in the past were mostly unavailable; still, they had enough, although standing there in the autumn sunshine was wearisome, and Moomi began to get fretful.

'Whose is that child, Lamia? I did not know you had a brother as young as that?'

Lamia turned; a girl whom she knew slightly had joined the queue behind her; she was in the class above her at school — a well-developed, dark-eyed beauty with raven hair that curled to her shoulders. She was quite a personage at school – President of the Debating Club and well known for her strong political views.

'He's my cousin's child,' said Lamia. 'Their house is in a dangerous position so he's staying with us.' In spite of her father's attempts to trace Moomi's relatives, she always liked to keep his identity secret. Just supposing – most unlikely, but just supposing – someone recognized him and took him! Then there would be nothing left at all.

'Moomi wants to get out,' he said suddenly.

'Moomi?' said Marcelle, laughing, 'What a strange name! What is it short for?'

Lamia hesitated and blushed. To give him his full name was to proclaim him a Moslem, for no Christian bore that name. Marcelle looked at her curiously and there was a short silence.

'It's just a nickname,' said Lamia at last.

'Well, I should choose another one then,' said Marcelle flatly. 'People are being shot down at the road-blocks for less than a name. Many are blotting out their religion or tearing up their identity cards altogether. And if you're harbouring a Moslem, you ought to give him back; we must all stand together in this, because it's the recognition of our faith that is at stake. This is a Holy War. What do you do in your spare time, Lamia?

'I study,' said Lamia, 'and I look after this . . . er . . . little boy. Also, we are still mourning; my brother was kidnapped and killed.'

'I'm sorry. I had not heard. But if they kidnapped and killed your brother, you must be longing to avenge him.'

'I am . . . but what can a girl do?'

They had reached the barrow and they were talking softly with their heads together. 'Come and see,' whispered Marcelle. 'You are just the sort of person we need. Come home with me and see what I do in my spare time.'

They moved on to their slow purchases, while Moomi,

released from the push chair, gathered acacia pods by the side of the road. Then, with their baskets full, they turned away together. Marcelle's house stood unsheltered, further to the west. The wall had been damaged by shellfire and the front windows were broken.

'Come in,' said Marcelle.

They met no one as they crossed the spacious hall and climbed the stairs to Marcelle's bedroom. There on the bed lay her battle-dress, beret and mask, and her rifle, ornamented with bright little pictures – a crucifix, the virgin mother and the Good Shepherd carrying a lamb on his shoulder.

'Many girls are now doing their part,' she said earnestly. 'We must hold our inheritance and our Christian faith. As I said before, this is a holy war, and the Church supports us. See, my Christ and my Holy Mother – they keep me safe.'

Moomi made a grab at the bright pictures, but Lamia picked him up and stood staring; the Good Shepherd caring for his sheep ... the inmates of that hotel buried alive under the rubble ... The Saviour hanging on the cross to save ... and the snipers shooting at the Fire Brigade and the ambulances which were trying to rescue the burnt and the wounded! Would the mother of Jesus have approved of what her children were doing and did the Good Shepherd not care? And what was this faith that they were defending? She tried to gather her confused thoughts, and of course it was a wonderful thing to fight for your country. How could she doubt it!

'Of course you are too young,' said Marcelle, 'but no one will know that you are only sixteen, you are so tall. Tell them you are seventeen; no one will bother to check. Come to my house at 6p.m. and I will take you to where the girls are training for the next round.'

'Thank you,' said Lamia, 'I will think about it.' She strapped Moomi into his pushchair and they went home.

Her father had not been back to the shop for two days. 'You would be mad to go into that quarter,' the voice of the radio had announced, so he waited. He sat slumped on the sofa, half asleep, and Lamia went and stood in front of him.

'Father,' she said quietly, 'I want to fight; girls are needed.'

He leaped to his feet and she thought he was going to strike her. 'Fight!' he shouted, 'My daughter fight! I'd rather shoot you myself than have you mown down by another man . . . and besides, do you know what happens to girls who are taken hostage? Fight indeed! Isn't it enough that our son threw away his life for a birthday party? . . . Have you no thought for your mother?'

Lamia fled in terror to the kitchen leaving Moomi to face the storm. He stood, legs apart, looking up at the furious man, interested but not afraid. He had heard so many storms and bangs in his young life and nothing had ever hurt him yet. 'Ah, Ba!' he said vigorously, and began marching up and down, clenching his fists and waving his arms in ridiculous imitation of Elias; until Elias, having made quite sure that the kitchen door was shut, began to laugh and subsided.

Lamia, having slammed the door, had flung herself down on a chair at the kitchen table and buried her face in her arms. Her father's rare rages might amuse Moomi but they upset her dreadfully. Her mother, sitting opposite her, started to cut up a cabbage and neither said anything at first. Moomi, finding little response from his Ba, wandered in and climbed on her lap and she hugged him tight because he was young and warm and vibrant. She glanced up at her mother, and thought how old and peaceful she looked concentrating on that cabbage – as though it mattered . . . and as though there was anything to be peaceful about.

'It's good to fight and protect one's country,' burst out Lamia at last. 'You and Father – you've had the best of your time. But we've got to grow up and live in it, and what about our children? Do you want them to grow up in a country where strangers have trampled on our inheritance and our faith? Isn't it right to protect them? You and Father are old; you don't understand.'

Her mother, aged 34, smiled a little and was silent. 'I wish she wouldn't wait so long before she speaks,' thought Lamia, 'and I wish she'd leave that cabbage alone.'

'I think that we shall live the best of our time in you and Sami and Huda and Moomi,' said Rosa, and she spoke slowly and haltingly as though feeling for words. 'But your future is a long time, I hope ... It is good to protect our faith ... but I think faith is best kept alive and protected in a heart that loves and forgives. I do not understand politics as you young ones do, but I listen and I see ... some men die in the mountains, so some women and children are murdered in the town ... Only yesterday I heard of a Moslem shot in the North ... so his fourteen-year-old brother took his gun and shot twelve Christian travellers at the road block ... and who, and how many will die for those twelve? Is this protecting our faith, or is it hate and revenge? ... and where does it stop? ... every truce is broken; no ceasefire lasts ...

'War does not last for ever; one day, perhaps, when all is destroyed, you who are left will turn and rebuild. In the village, in my girlhood, I would watch them ploughing the ground and sowing the seed before the winter ... then in the spring, the harvests appeared and the fields were green ...

'You have taken this child, Lamia; one of our enemies. When he is grown, maybe the storm will have passed and the time for rebuilding will have come ... prepare him now for that day; teach him our faith ... Teach him to love and forgive. Look forward to the harvest beyond the winter.

Perhaps this is the greatest thing we women can do for our country.'

But for Lamia it was useless to look forward. She could see nothing at all beyond the black smoke-screen by day and the red glare of the burning at night.

7

And then, quite suddenly, after several days and nights of bombardment, when the parched ground was crying out for the first rains and the land wilted under the October sun, a ceasefire was proclaimed, and this time men prophesied that it would hold, for the leaders of the chief warring parties had returned from Syria with new conditions of peace.

Pandemonium reigned; people wept, some for joy and some for sorrow because of the wasted lives and senseless killings that had achieved nothing. The barricades in the streets were overthrown as though they were objects of hate, and men who had been sniping at each other a few hours before came out into the open and hugged and kissed each other amid the rubble and ruin, and wound great wreaths of crimson purple bougainvillaea round their rifles. 'Peace has come,' cried the citizens gathered round their radios in their homes, and many lifted up their heads and praised God for their living families, while the children ran out laughing into the sunshine and freedom of safe streets. It was a Saturday and they were all at home.

'Peace!' cried Huda, dancing round the house, shining-eyed. 'Now we can play in the groves and I can sleep in my own bedroom every night.'

'Peace,' sighed Sami, 'and Father never let me go near a real battle or fire a gun.' He seized Huda's hand and they ran off to join the celebrations in the village streets.

'Peace,' thought Rosa, 'and now my husband will come home at normal hours and I shall not fear for him all day long. We too must celebrate when he arrives.' There was not much food in the house, but Rosa could make a little go a long way and she made straight for the kitchen. Moomi, suspecting a baking, followed her.

'Peace,' thought Lamia, 'and at what price? Was it for this he died?' She suddenly felt an intolerable longing to be near her brother, and although she knew she should have been helping her mother, she walked out of the house and took the path that led to the cemetery. There were no flowers now; only the colour of the drought — silver of olive leaves, pale gold of stubble field, and above her the crimson and bronze of the stripped vineyards. The church stood like a grey rock jutting from the mountainside, but she did not go in. She had never been in since Amin died, because the pale Christ on the cross, and his mournful faced mother with her eyes uplifted had not answered her prayer any more than any other bits of wood and plaster. 'I think I'm an atheist now,' she thought rather vaguely, and her deep sense of loneliness increased because it was terrible to believe that there was no one there at all. She entered the cemetery and slipped between the cypresses; then her heart seemed to miss a beat, for she was not alone after all. Hanni sat beside the grave, his head bowed in an attitude of deep dejection, and Lamia suddenly forgot that she had despised him, for here was someone who cared deeply. As she ran across the grass towards him, he looked up, and she noticed the thinness of his face and his sunken dark-rimmed eyes. He looked as though he had not slept for weeks.

'Hanni!'

He gave a weary little smile. 'I thought you might come here,' he said. 'I couldn't imagine you jigging and prancing in the streets with the others, and the grass not yet sprung up on the graves.'

She was silent for a time, digesting his words. She had not seen him since the last outbreak of fighting but she knew he had been at the hospital; and now, on this day of celebration, he had come to sit by this hard-baked plot of earth and he had expected to meet her there. It was as though something had been said, at last, that had bridged the silence between them for ever, and she hardly knew how to go on.

'You have been at the hospital all this time?' she queried. She sat on the ground beside him, clasping her knees.

'Yes, I could not leave.'

'What was it like, Hanni? Was it very busy?'

'Day and night; they lay waiting on stretchers. By the time we got to them it was often too late. And sometimes the Palestinians would rush in their wounded and make us treat them at gunpoint, while others, more needy, died.'

'You treated all sides then?'

'Of course. Does death take sides? Did that rocket that exploded in the bread queue? Fifty died, mostly women and children. Are the parents of those children dancing and embracing their enemies today? Lamia, I'm beginning to feel I can't stand any more of it — the screams, the blood, the look in their eyes! What have they done? What are these sufferings achieving?'

He was shuddering, pressing his hand to his forehead. She watched him, horrified, longing to comfort him, not knowing what to say.

'But you won't have to stand it any longer, Hanni?' she faltered. 'It is finished. This peace will hold; everybody says so.'

'Finished?' he repeated savagely, 'What's finished? Have the mothers finished weeping or the orphans finished mourning? Is your sorrow finished? You come to the hospital, Lamia, and you will see lives that are just beginning — lives that will never walk or see or understand again ... vegetable lives; I wish they *were* finished ... besides, who says this peace will hold? How many other cease-fires have we seen? Have they held?'

'They say this one is different,' she murmured miserably

and fell silent. There was no comfort anywhere, except in this frail new understanding, this shared mood. They sat quietly, both conscious of it, until the clouds massed behind the mountain and hid the sun. It was suddenly cold and they rose to go.

'If only the rain would come,' said Hanni bleakly. 'The city stinks of death and the rubbish is rotting in the streets.'

They set off for home and Huda saw them and ran to meet them, eyes sparkling, curls flying, with Moomi staggering along far behind.

'Come quick, Lamia; Mother has made a feast and Father is home. We are all waiting for you. Hanni, come and drink coffee with us.'

He shrugged his shoulders. 'I'll wait till I see whether there's anything to feast about first,' he said, and stared moodily at Moomi, who had just arrived, warm and joyful, his cheeks crimson, his forehead damp with perspiration. He held out his arms and Lamia lifted him on to her hip although he was getting terribly heavy, and Hanni stared moodily at him almost as though he hated him. 'Perhaps he's jealous,' thought Lamia, 'or perhaps he's seeing these other children . . . I wish I could comfort him . . .' She turned to him, no longer shy, her expression gentle and understanding, but it was too late, he was already hurrying down the track that led to the village, and when she called after him, he took no notice.

The family gathered round the table, amazed at what Rosa had produced from the meagre rations of past weeks eked out by things from the garden, and Lamia was conscious of the interplay of thought and feeling that flowed between her parents. Elias sat moody and passive. 'How can you feast when the rains have not even fallen on our son's grave?' he seemed to be saying as he stared toward the mountain; while Rosa glanced first at him and then at the children – at Moomi, shining-eyed at the sight of so many goodies; at Huda jogging up and down in her seat; at Sami, his cheeks already bulging with food although no one else had started. 'Let them be happy today,' she seemed to be pleading. 'Our hearts have died, but they still have far to go. Let them live again in joy!' And gradually the joy of the children prevailed and they drew together and talked about the old days before the killings had started. Rosa told tales of feasting in the village, when the corn was cut and the grapes and the olives harvested. They sat round the open window for the weather was sultry, and Moomi, sleepy with food, rested on Elias's lap. It was an evening they would always remember, like a bright rift in the storm clouds. It was so quiet; perhaps, when the rain came and the grass on the mountain turned green, they would all start to live again. They sat till long after dark, and then Huda went to bed in her own little room with her windows open towards the sea, and the rest of the family too slept deeply and gratefully, and woke to peace.

But only for a few hours; they all heard it at once . . . the thunder of the guns and the roar of the explosives, and Elias leaned over and switched on the radio. Huda ran crying into her mother's arms, and Sami looked thoughtful. Even though he had lost a brother, the sound of battle still stirred his blood in a not unpleasant way. He longed to grow up.

It was all over. A right-wing official was missing – where or why, nobody knew. But it was enough to trigger off the guns. The wreaths, the embracing and dancing were all forgotten, and the city was plunged into the fiercest phase of fighting that it had yet experienced. The battle was raging in the western quarter, and to the north of Elias's home, and business was now impossible. The great hotels had become fortresses under siege and hundreds were dying. Those who lived in those areas were evacuating with what they could carry, some escaping over the rooftops with the bullets singing past their ears. Families were stranded in cellars for days on end, and, even on the outskirts, food and water were scarce. Looting was so severe that men hired armed guards to protect their homes and paid huge sums to the different political parties to leave them alone.

Elias forbade the children to leave the house and Rosa tried to organize some sort of routine. Lamia taught the younger children in the mornings and plodded on with her own studies in the afternoon, but they were bored and irritable and in spite of the sultry weather the rains had not yet fallen. Only Rosa was never irritable, and only Moomi was never bored. He was always busy when there was nothing to do, eager in the hottest, dullest hours, laughing when there was nothing whatever to laugh about, and Lamia continued to wonder how they would ever have faced life without him.

One night they were sleeping, accustomed to the rumble of the bombardment, when a tremendous explosion rocked the house and blasted the western windows. They were sleeping, as usual, in the rooms that faced the mountain, which was a mercy as Huda's little bed was covered with great jagged pieces of broken glass. They leaped up, the children clinging to their parents, who calmed them as best they could.

'Stay near the front door,' said Elias, 'I will go and see what has happened.

He went to the back of the house, but came back quickly. 'It's the apartment blocks behind us,' he said. 'A stray mortar must have exploded right inside and the flames are shooting through the windows. The people are swarming like ants; I suppose they were all sleeping on the ground floor – but they had better not come here; it's too close for safety. Let's collect what we can, in case our house catches fire.'

They all worked hard. There was the space of the long garden and the street between the buildings, and fortunately the wind was blowing from the east. When they had collected all they could carry, they ran up to the roof for a few moments and watched the great flames leaping skyward, blown toward the city. Then they went back to the front room and huddled miserably, ready for flight, Huda sobbing bitterly because all her dolls and teddies had not been considered necessary for survival.

Rosa made coffee and the older members of the family watched the stained dawn break through a haze of grey smoke. Weary and white-faced, they climbed to the roof a second time. The great building had fallen in and the flames no longer leaped; they burned sullenly, pale against the crimson east, and Elias's own home stood starkly unprotected, a target on a hillside, and the ruined city seemed to lie at their feet.

'It seems quiet enough now,' said Elias at last. 'I'm going to the shop to bring what I can. We may not be able to stay here long now; I'll eat when I return.'

He set off, dodging the enemy quarters and road blocks. His mind was absorbed in this new problem, but even so, he smelt the bitter smell of burning a long way off. He parked his car in the usual place, and walked to the narrow back street guessing what he would find, for the thick air choked him and made his eyes water. As he turned the corner he saw what he already knew; the whole street had burned; every little shop was gutted or looted and bales of spoiled material lay in the ashes. He picked his way over the debris and stood gazing at the black shell of his own shop. First his son, and now his shop. He felt ashamed that he should think of them together, but it had been his father's shop, his past as his son had been his future. Now past and future were destroyed and he stood suspended, disconnected, in this nightmare present. There was nothing to salvage; he stumbled back to his car and somehow found his way home.

But there was the present; the rest of the family were fast asleep, but Rosa heard his horn and came to the door. She looked small and pale in her black dress, but she was there. She was always there when he needed her, dutiful and submissive, but at the same time, his rock in the storm, his peace. Through all the strain and sorrow, she had never gone under or given in and he was conscious of a great rush of grateful love which he knew he would never express, not being a demonstrative man. He greeted her in his usual quiet fashion.

'The shop has gone,' he said. 'There was nothing to salvage. They've gutted the street.'

She looked at him. She knew how he felt about his shop. There was nothing to say so she went into the kitchen and came back with a loaded tray and a letter in her hand. She sat beside him and waited quietly till he had eaten.

'I've had a letter from my uncle in Damour,' she said at last. 'His son is fighting and brought it by hand. He could not stop. His parents have gone to Cyprus to wait until things improve. They have offered us their house till they return. They are afraid of leaving it empty. It is quieter there to the south and the house is up on the hillside away from the coast road and well sheltered.'

'There's nothing to stay for now,' he replied. 'And this house is an easy target. We'd better go. I'll leave an armed guard here and we'll take all we can.'

'Of course, we could go to my parents in the village,' she said wistfully.

He smiled; her love of village life always amused him.

'How could we live?' he asked, 'and there would be no advanced schooling for Lamia. No, your uncle's house in

Damour would be better. I have some of my goods stored here in the house, and I might start up business again down there.'

She stared across to where the poplars burned gold above Amin's grave. Her husband did not know how often she sat in the window and gazed at that grave.

'Yes,' she said. 'I suppose we'd better go.'

8

They moved to the south of the city within a couple of weeks during a lull in the fighting. While they were packing up the clouds broke and the first rains fell in torrents. It was the time of year that Lamia had always loved, that meeting of life and death and both equally beautiful; when the trees and bushes flamed into autumn colours and a veil of green seemed to fall suddenly over the parched land. When Rosa went on a last visit to the cemetery she found wild crocuses flowering all round the grave.

And just as the earth cried out for water, so the torn land cried out for peace, and there came a day when the radio called for a March of Peace, and thousands responded. Moslems, Druze, and Christians poured into the streets weeping and crying out their hatred of violence and their desperation. Priests and sheikhs and imams led together, their enmity forgotten, in this heart-cry for peace. Bells rang out from church towers, and from the mosques and minarets muezzins chanted verses from the Koran, and called for tolerance, forgiveness, and understanding. Sami was away and in the thick of it before anyone had decided whether he could go or not, and it was the most thrilling thing he had ever done in his life. Not even the gunmen at the checkpoints could stop them. That mighty mass of anguished people, many of them bereaved and many of them with their homes in ruins, had brushed them aside. For a few days it seemed that the fourth round was over, and Elias hired a van and moved his family and property while the streets were relatively safe.

The children settled quickly into their new home, and if Rosa and Lamia felt the limitations of a much smaller house, they made the best of it, for there were several advantages. The nights were quieter and Sami and Huda could go to school again. On those warm November Saturday afternoons they could even run through the orange groves to play on the beach, and Rosa would walk down to meet them, for she was never quite happy when they were out of her sight. So many children in those days had run out of their houses to play and had never come home again.

It was the season of rain and sun, of stormy sunsets and great rainbows flung over the sea from Sidon to the city. Elias had started up a small business to the north of the little town and the stricken family seemed to pause, draw a deep breath, and start again. Christmas was coming, and perhaps, once again, the lights would shine, the bells would ring, and there would be peace on earth and goodwill to men.

And then once again the ugly rumours began and people huddled round their radios, cold with fear. A lorry load of Korans had been overturned and the books burned, so churches had been vandalised and war had broken out in the mountains. Four bodies of the Christian Party were found outside a village and the retaliations in the city were so brutal, and so many innocent Moslems were massacred, that the day became known as Black Saturday. By Monday, the whole centre of the city was in a state of fierce war, and for eight days burning, shelling and kidnapping raged in the battle area. Then Syria pressed for another ceasefire and the shooting ceased, and once again the task of burying the dead began. But on that very same day attacks started in the mountains to the north and southeast, and scores of homeless families, shouldering their babies and their few vital necessities of life, started their treks over the dangerous, gun-ridden hill country to they knew not where. For the land was beginning to be divided into hard and fast partitions, and each party and religion gravitated towards its own.

And now, to Huda, came the worst news of all: there was to be no Christmas. Christmas, to her, was the most wonderful day in the year, and her Christmases shone out like bright jewels strung across the eight years of her life. Last year, her father had taken them all to the main shopping centre of the city; the streets had been brightly lit and decorated and carols blared out from a loud speaker. They had bought golden cardboard caskets of chocolates and sugar almonds and driven home to a feast round a lighted tree and a little home-made crib. But this year the rubbish was piled high in the shopping centre, the shops closed, and the streets at night deserted of all except the snipers. So there would be no Christmas, no tree, no gifts, no crib, nothing at all except prayers for peace. The church had said so, and you could not argue with the church.

Huda was a strange looking little girl. Her hair grew in a black thatch, and her small face seemed mostly great black eyes. She was very thin, with bony, spindly legs and gave the impression of being top-heavy. She stood in front of her mother in the kitchen, her fists clenched, her eyes huge and tragic.

'I want Christmas,' she whispered passionately. 'I want the tree and the candles and the Christ Child.'

Rosa smoothed back her unruly hair and smiled down at her. It was important to obey the church, but there were other things even more important.

'You can go and get a fir bough on Christmas Eve,' she promised, 'and we'll light the candles. I think we left the Christ Child behind, but perhaps your doll will do. Don't tell anyone. It will be a secret little Christmas for you and Sami and Moomi.'

So that was why she and Moomi were hurrying up the hillside to the spinney at about quarter past three on Christmas Eve, a quiet cold day, when the snow had fallen on the Lebanon Range. They had not far to go, and Rosa could watch them all the way from the window, if she looked out. But she was busy cooking little gingerbread stars in the kitchen, and she did not see the girl sitting beside the path with her head in her hands. Huda, always inquisitive, stopped and stared at her.

'What's the matter?' she asked. 'Are you ill?'

The girl looked up. She was young, probably still in her teens, and her eyes were full of fear.

'Who are you, child?' she asked. 'Are you Moslem or Christian?'

'I'm a Christian,' said Huda proudly, 'but Moomi's not a Christian. He came from the camp.'

The girl glanced at Moomi. He had found a little puddle and had made a mud pie. His hands were black and his face was streaked with dirt. He did not look in the least like a Christian.

'Then why is he with you?' asked the girl.

'My sister found him . . .' Huda broke off suddenly, remembering that Lamia had forbidden her to tell. But she need not have worried. The girl suddenly doubled up with a little moan and the sweat broke out on her forehead.

'Whatever's the matter?' asked Huda, frightened. 'If you are ill you had better come home with me. My mother will look after you.'

The girl relaxed slowly and drew a long breath.

'Yes, and your father would shoot me, I expect. Your people burned and destroyed most of the houses in our village and my husband has disappeared. I thought I could get to my parents in Sidon, but my time has come sooner than I expected. I'd rather have my baby out here alone on the hillside than die at their hands, but I ran from a blazing house and I have nothing to wrap it in . . . and nothing to eat. Little girl, do you think, for the love of God, you could help me?'

'Are you going to have a baby?' asked Huda, deeply interested. 'Of course, I'll help you and so will my mother. But I've got to run up to the wood first and get a Christmas tree, because it's Christmas Eve. I shan't be long.'

The girl seized her skirt. There was panic in her eyes.

'Little girl, never mind about the Christmas tree. If your mother's willing to help a Druze girl, tell her to come now. It's cold for a new baby out on the hillside and I want him to live. He's all I have. Run, child, in the name of God, run!'

Huda hesitated. The Christmas tree was the most important part of Christmas, and if she did not get it now she would never get it at all. Already the winter sun hung low over the calm sea. Dusk came quickly and she would not be allowed out again. But this girl seemed very ill and she did not want the baby to die.

'Come on, Moomi,' she said seizing his hand, and fighting back her tears she dragged him back to the house and arrived breathless. Even in her excitement she noticed the fragrant smell of baking; quite ordinary baking, but in those days even quite ordinary things seemed rare and beautiful.

'Mother,' she gasped, 'there's a girl. She's a Druze and she says you'll shoot her. She's going to have a baby and she's nothing to wrap it up in and nothing to eat. Mother, Father wouldn't shoot her, would he?'

'Where is this girl, Huda?' Rosa was already putting on her coat. 'Take me to her at once! Lamia, watch the oven.'

Moomi also stayed to watch the oven and Rosa and Huda hurried up the hill. The sun was just disappearing over the horizon making a gold track across the sea. 'When I can swim,' thought Huda, 'I'll swim up that track and the water will shine all round me.'

The girl lay on the grass, her face ashen, her eyes terrified with pain and the fear of her enemies, but when she saw Rosa the fear died away. She knew at once, that for the time being at least, they were neither Druze, nor Moslem, nor Christian; just two mothers fighting for a precious life.

'How often are the pains coming?' asked Rosa. 'And can you walk if I help you? Huda, bring the bundle, and let's try.'

It was quite a big bundle, and Huda's last hope faded. She had still thought that it might have been possible to run very fast in the dusk and seize a branch while her mother talked to the girl, but there was nothing for it but to obey. She picked up the bundle and they started home very slowly, stopping twice on the way when the spasms of pain came on. But they reached the house at last and Rosa disappeared into the bedroom with the girl and shut the door. Lamia was washing up; Elias and Sami were playing draughts. There was no tree, no candles, no crib, no Christmas and no mother. Huda flung herself down on her bed and, like many other children in the land that year, wept for her spoiled Christmas. She must have fallen asleep with all her clothes on, for she was woken, as it seemed to her, in the middle of the night by Lamia shaking her. 'Come Huda,' whispered Lamia, 'wake up and come quick. It's Christmas, but you mustn't tell anyone.'

Somehow Huda staggered downstairs, supported by her sister, tousled and dazed with sleep. At the entrance of the living room she stopped and blinked at six lighted candles shining at the base of a little tree. There was a low table with a red cloth, and on it, plates of biscuits shaped like stars, sparkling glasses and a jug of mulberry juice. All the family were waiting for her and in the centre of the group was a basket, and in the basket a new-born baby, washed and fragrant, its dark hair still damp.

Huda ran into her mother's arms, half-dreaming, half awake. 'But there wasn't a Christmas tree,' she babbled. 'I couldn't go . . . and we left the Christ Child behind . . . He was in the top drawer of the big cupboard . . . Mother, is this the Christ Child? Did he come by himself? Oh Mother, this is the loveliest Christmas we've ever had!'

Everyone laughed softly, so as not to wake the baby. 'Yes, I think he did come,' said Rosa rather vaguely. She had never had a Bible of her own and she did not know that Jesus had said, 'Whosoever receives one such child in my name receives me,' but there was something here that she could not quite account for.

'Can we start on the biscuits?' whispered Sami. 'And shall I pour out the mulberry juice?'

Rosa looked round, puzzled; at Elias, who had braved the dusk and the curfew to fetch a little tree for Huda; at Lamia cuddling a sleepy Moomi; at the candlelight reflected in the starry eyes of Sami and Huda; at the crumpled baby. She thought of the girl in the next room, sleeping unafraid and sheltered. They were all here, Druze, Palestinian and Christian. Outside there raged what would soon be called the ugliest war in history, but in this small circle of candlelight, with the baby in the midst, there was peace on earth and goodwill to men.

9

Christmas passed and a few days later Elias drove the girl and her baby to the border of her Druze district, from where she could walk in safety to her parents' house, but, as far as Huda was concerned, the baby never really went away. Life, for her, had been at its lowest ebb with Amin dead and the candles darkened and the carols silenced; but you can't quench Christmas, and so the baby had arrived just in time. And, as in the Nativity scenes painted by the old masters all the light seems to stream from the Infant's face, so, to Huda, the baby in the basket had been the source of all their Christmas joy and togetherness. She was only eight years old, and the boundary between reality and fantasy not yet very well defined, so, to her, the baby was no enemy refugee, but the Christ Child come to them. She had known many frightening, sorrowful hours in the past months and, if the grown-ups spoke truth, there was worse coming; but from now onwards he would always be there, lighting the candles in the dark and drawing them together. Secure in his presence, she seemed as gay and carefree as Moomi, and Rosa smiled and wondered what had happened to her little daughter.

The new year crept in, uncelebrated and without rejoicing, although Elias congratulated himself, and Rosa thanked God, that they had moved from their old district. The Palestinians were holding the roads that led east, and the suburbs around them, including their own, had become a great scarred, burning battlefield. The sixth round of the war had started with renewed violence. There was fighting in the north, fighting along the Damascus Road, fighting on the sea-front, and fighting in the mountains, while on one grey January morning Moslems marched from the Sidon area in the south to the help of their allies in the city, attacking the Maronite towns that stood in the way. Rosa and Lamia first heard of it when Sami rushed into the house, his eyes shining, and announced that Palestinian troops were marching along the coast road, and fighting had already broken out. He had watched from the roof of his friend's house and seen the first explosions. He had just come to tell them . . . he must get back.

But Rosa and Lamia seized him at the same time by his shirt, and Lamia shook him till he yelled. 'If you leave this house again,' she threatened, 'Father will thrash you within an inch of your life.' Sami believed her and retired sulkily to his room to revel in the distant roar and smoke of the bombardment. He also saw his father hurrying home from the shop, pale and anxious, and a moment or two later Sami was ordered to come down, sharply enough. Only at night, when the younger children were in bed, did Elias, Rosa, and Lamia climb to the roof and watch the blaze of battle along the dark coast road. They had been discussing the possibility of moving up to the mountains where Rosa's parents lived, but had decided against it. The roads were dangerous, the villages were being attacked, and the fighting was still a long way off.

'Our house is well off the road, and well protected from rockets and shrapnel,' said Elias. 'If they start attacking the town we can flee to the mountains from the back; but then we lose all, and how shall we live? Besides we promised to guard our uncle's house.'

'As you will, my husband,' said Rosa rather sadly. She saw the sense of it, but she longed for her old parents these days; she had had no news of them for many weeks.

They slept fitfully and spent most of the next day

huddled round the radio. Their own Party Leader, the Minister of the Interior, was directing the defence against the oncoming army from his own sea-side palace nearby, but even so, the terrible sounds of war seemed to be coming nearer. Many had fled at the outset, but few dared to leave the house now, for the town appeared to be in a state of siege. Food would be scarce, and Rosa eked out the rations and tried to cheer the bored, restless children. Lamia was a bundle of nerves, Huda scared and tearful, and Sami rebelliously straining to escape. Only Moomi remained happy and contented and Lamia clung to him as to a lifeline, half starving herself so that he would have plenty and holding him through the rowdy nights when sleep was impossible.

The noisy days passed; Elias betook himself and his gun to the rooftop at the end of the road and, like many others, kept guard over his own street, only coming home for food and snatches of sleep. He was not there on the fourth day, when the sudden deafening roar of planes flying low, sent them all rushing into a corner of the room where Rosa sat knitting. They clung to her, terrified, while the thunder of the engines mingled with the scream and crash of high explosives. Elias burst into the house, white-faced and shaken.

'They are bombarding the enemy supply lines,' he gasped. 'Maybe now they will have to withdraw.'

'Then had we not better leave?' shouted Rosa.

He hesitated, for he knew it was too late; he had hoped for the best too long. From his rooftop shelter, squatting with his gun, he had watched the troops surround the town ready to shoot on sight, and no one could leave now. The intervention of the Lebanese Air Force might save them, but nothing else would.

'We can't go out in this bombing,' he shouted. 'Perhaps later. Have you made bundles of what we can carry? The

76

car is still hidden out in the trees, but it's bitterly cold outside. Each child should bring a blanket and whatever food we can carry. In the meantime we will go down into the basement; there is nothing to be done while this raid is on.'

There was nothing to be done any more. The bundles were ready for flight but flight had become impossible. The planes withdrew, but the great bombardment was coming closer, the crash of glass and falling masonry more frequent. They collected all they needed for the night and went down into the basement. The house was built on a slope and this small, cave-like room opened on to a back alley and was used to store tools and potatoes and grain. From the tiny back window they could see the glare of the burning and the hot fog of smoke; but inside it was dark and cool and smelt of earth and paraffin.

'What shall we do if the house catches fire?' shivered Sami.

'We shall go out of the back door with our bundles,' said Rosa. She spoke very calmly and her peace seemed to be holding them all steady. She could not understand it herself, for she knew now that they were all trapped. Perhaps, when Amin died, she had passed through the horror of death and somehow reached the haven beyond the storm. Lamia, her own body alternately hot and cold with fear, huddled against her with Moomi, trustful and interested, clasped close, for he had never known a world without big bangs and it seemed normal to him. Huda snuggled in her mother's lap and Sami sat, wide-eyed, in the crook of his father's arm. At last, he was actually beginning to dislike war.

They sat for a long time, unable to hear themselves speak, and then Rosa proposed supper and went upstairs briefly. There was very little bread left, but there were cold potatoes, olives, tins of sardines and some biscuits. They heated water on a primus, because the electricity had failed, and made coffee. After supper they lit the candles and it reminded Huda of Christmas and she cheered up.

The bombardment lasted all night. Elias stayed with the family for one could not snipe against these great exploding missiles. While the children slept, in the small hours of the morning he lay cursing himself for his fatal optimism and lack of foresight. 'How shall we live?' he had asked; now he was beginning to wonder, 'How shall we die?' and, as though she guessed his thoughts, Rosa moved over beside him and reached out to him across Sami.

'You are awake, my husband?'

'Of course; who could sleep in this hell? Rosa, I'm sorry. We should have left three days ago.'

'It was not your fault, Elias; how could you know that it would move so fast?'

'If there is a lull, we might still get away, unless the car has been stolen or smashed. It was well hidden.'

'Yes, if there is a lull I think we should try and get away in the dark. It's Lamia I worry about most. She is so beautiful, and they do terrible things to girls.'

'It's not only the girls; you, too, are beautiful. But don't worry. If they come to rape you or Lamia, I shall shoot you both with my own gun, before they shoot me.'

'But what about our little children?'

'They will not spare us for our children — nor do I think they will shoot such young children. I think they will go to the nuns like all the others. They will be kindly cared for, if they live.'

He lifted Sami out of the way and took her in his arms, and she thrilled to his touch as a bride might, for never before had he told her that she was beautiful. And Lamia, woken by the strangeness of a five-minute silence, heard what her father said, and lay marvelling. He would shoot her himself, rather than see her raped or mutilated, and die content, with her. Her silent father had always cared for her and provided for her, but now she knew, for the first time, how deeply he loved her. For love is a strange plant. It may grow unnoticed and unrecognised on the sunny slopes and only break into flower in the valley of the shadow of death.

They knew it was morning by the grey square of light in the little back window, and they rose stiffly, no one wanting to be the first to look out on the stark tragedy of the night. The great bombardment seemed to be over; Rosa went to collect some breakfast, Sami was asking when he could go out and collect some shrapnel for his war museum, and Elias went cautiously to the door. He came back immediately, his face grey with fear and seized his gun.

'They have broken right into the town,' he said to Rosa. 'I can hear the shouting, and the rattle of guns, and the screams of those who are being massacred. Some are running in the streets but they are shooting after them. I will go back and watch from behind the parapet, but you, all of you, go down to the basement and lie very still under the blankets. If they come, they may not see you. Just lie very very still.'

He kissed Rosa and left her. She collected some bottles of water, a little food and her rosary and crucifix. She also found a bottle of sleeping tablets, left over from some previous illness; she dissolved two in a little warm milk and coaxed Moomi to drink them, and in ten minutes he was deeply asleep, sweating freely. Then she hurried the children down into the basement again, made them lie down, and piled blankets, rugs and sacks on top of them. Finally she crept in beside them, leaving a small opening for air.

Elias soon joined them. 'It is useless to resist,' he

whispered. 'They are pouring along the streets. It would only draw attention to the house. Listen! You can hear them.'

They lay like statues; they could all hear it now, for it was coming very near: the savage Moslem war cry, 'God is great, God is great!' They screamed it as they shot, they yelled it over men, women and children who lay in huddled heaps, or died, clinging together in their little homes. Sometimes they could hear the sound of running feet along the alley, and sometimes the cries receded and sometimes they seemed very near. The family lay, hour after hour, sweating and trembling and time seemed unreal, for down there in the dark only life and death were real and the intense awareness that they had of each other. All these years, up to a point, they had taken each other for granted, but now their eyes were opened and every moment together seemed precious.

'Ba,' whispered Sami suddenly, 'will they just shoot us, or will it be worse?'

No one answered. Rosa soothed him and gave him a drink of water; it seemed as though years of time had rolled over them and the stiffness and stuffiness were becoming unbearable. Then the sounds they dreaded suddenly erupted, very close at hand; the cries, the shots and the sudden silences. And, to make matters worse, Moomi stirred and whimpered and showed every sign of waking up.

The end came quite suddenly. They had expected an attack on the front door, but there was a rush of feet in the alley behind, a bullet shot through the bolt and the door flew open. Men burst in, but their voices were almost too weary and hoarse to announce that God was great any longer. Someone gave orders and someone butted savagely at the blankets with the muzzle of his gun, pushing it down onto Moomi's ear so that the child gave a muffled scream.

With a shout of triumph, the soldiers flung back the coverings and ordered their victims to stand against the wall and hold up their hands. Elias hesitated and his hand stole to his gun.

But Rosa was before him; she seized Moomi, and holding him in front of her, she walked straight towards the loaded barrel. 'Shoot us if you must,' she said, 'but spare your own. This is a Palestinian child; my daughter found him under his mother's body in the orange groves above the camp, six months ago, and has cared for him ever since. Surely you will not kill your own.'

There was a deathly silence. The man in charge seemed to be a soldier of some rank for he motioned the others to fall back and stood staring and staring. The smoky yellow light of a winter evening fell on the face of the half-drugged child, and Moomi also stared through his tears. Old forgotten memories stirred; except for the past eight months, his whole baby life had been spent among fierce men who waved guns and shouted and smelt of explosive, and he felt thoroughly at home with this black-bearded desperado in his blood-stained, smoke-blackened uniform. He held out his arms and murmured dreamily, 'ah Ba!'

'What is his name?' whispered the solider, through dry lips.

'Moomi,' said the child, yawning. 'Ah Ba!'

'Moomi!'

The officer handed his gun to a soldier in the doorway and took the child, who fell asleep instantly, his head on the strange man's shoulder. Then he pulled up the damp shirt, and stood as though mesmerized, staring at the purple birthmark on Moomi's back.

'The child of the evil eye!' he muttered, 'Abdel Moomin! My sister's child! It is he! Our mother weeps for him every day.' He turned to Rosa. 'Tell me again, where and when you found him.'

'My daughter will tell you,' said Rosa, turning back to Lamia. But the girl had fainted and was lying ashen-faced on the floor, with Elias kneeling beside her. Sami and Huda stood obediently with their arms in the air, their eyes huge with terror.

'Put them down,' said Rosa calmly, 'no one is going to hurt you.' They slumped, exhausted, onto the blanket and she turned back to the officer.

'We advertised for his people,' she said, 'but there was no reply. We found him three days after you killed my son. But we did not kill your sister's son and had I found your sister alive, I would have cared for her, too. Let us take him to our parents' village in the mountain, and from there his people can come and claim him. Is his father alive?'

The man scowled. 'My brother was wounded on Black Saturday, less than a month ago,' he muttered. 'I shall avenge his injuries. Nevertheless, for the sake of the child, I will spare you. His life for yours! I will set a guard on the house. Stay here till I return.'

He handed back the now unconscious Moomi and went out closing the door. No one spoke. Rosa set about restoring Lamia with a cold handkerchief. The girl opened her eyes and looked round just as a burning building flared up and by the dull orange glow, she could see all her family sitting round her; her head was cradled on her mother's lap and they were no longer suffocating and sweating, but they were breathing relatively fresh air. She thought they must all have been shot and gone to Paradise together, but why was the light so dim, and why were they all so grave and quiet, and why should Moomi snore so loudly in Paradise? She gave it up and shut her eyes and her mother held water to her lips and stroked her hair.

They stayed there for hours and even ate a little food and tried to rest. In the small hours of the night there was a lull of utter exhaustion and the children slept. Then the silence was broken by quick footsteps, the door was flung open and the officer waved a torch above them.

'Follow me,' he said, 'and hurry!'

'We have our car hidden up in the trees,' said Rosa boldly, 'and we want to go to the village. Will you escort us in safety?'

'It is impossible,' said the man roughly. 'Every car lamp is a target. It's raining, and you cannot negotiate the hill paths without light in this weather. You must go down to the Minister's Palace on the coast and you must hurry for it will soon be bombed. You must go through the orange groves; thousands are seeking refuge and fishing boats are taking them up north. From the northern port you must make your way to your mother's house in the village in the Metn, and the child's grandmother will come for him when there is a lull in the fighting. It is not safe for a man to travel up there. Now, come.'

Elias picked up Huda, Rosa carried Moomi, while Lamia and Sami hoisted bundles on their backs and they stepped out into the ghost town. The noise had prepared them for much, but not for this; fires still spluttered in the rain as they hurried along after their guide, scrambling over great heaps of rubble, stumbling over dead bodies, or bodies that still moaned feebly. The smell of death and burning hung on the dark and the night, the rain and the temporary silence made it all the more eerie. At the end of the valley the soldier stopped. He lifted his lantern to scan them and they could see his stained face and bloodshot eyes.

'Swear by God that you'll give him back,' he croaked.

'If she comes and can prove that he is hers, then I swear by God,' replied Rosa.

'How will she prove it?' His restless hand moved to the trigger of his gun.

'She must know the date her daughter disappeared. And

is there no photo?'

'Perhaps,' muttered the soldier, 'and we know the day of our sister's death. But if you refuse . . .' he uttered a fearful oath, and disappeared into the black shambles.

When they reached the end of the valley, they realised they were not alone. Hundreds more were pressing on through the mud and rain with children in their arms, or carrying the wounded or the very old on improvised stretchers. No one spoke or glanced at anyone else; there was little time to lose for they had to cross the coast road before the fighting started again.

It was still and quiet when they crossed and the salt wind from the sea blew the rain into their eyes as they struggled into the orange groves. They had hoped for more shelter here, but the trees had been stripped of their fruit and leaves and the spoiled boughs shivered against the cold grey of a January dawn. When at last they arrived at the palace by the sea, soaked and unutterably weary, there was no room to enter and they crouched in the shelter of the verandah. Five thousand were to find refuge there and many were leaving by small craft sailing north and others by helicopter.

A group of men sat, disconsolate, on the ground leaning against the wall. Their eyes were dark and hopeless and they glanced at Elias indifferently.

'You had better push your wife and children to the front,' said one. 'I think they will soon bombard the palace; mine have just left.'

Rosa stared at him. Something sounded wrong.

'Then why have you not gone with them?' she asked.

'Because they are not taking the men. We must escape as we may, and we probably shan't. Only women and children are being taken into the boats.'

'Then go quickly,' said Elias almost roughly, 'and wait at the northern port. There will be some accommodation there for refugees. I will get back to the hills and please

God, I will find a way to come to you. If I do not come in three days, then don't wait any longer. Go up to the village.'

'Because I shall be lying in the mud with a bullet through me,' he thought to himself, and he had never felt so alone in his life before. 'Rosa, Rosa!'

She turned her back on the children and came to him. Lying in that stuffy shelter, something had happened to their marriage. She had gone back in time and watched the years unfolding as though in a film. She had been brought to him eighteen years ago, a scared little country child-bride, and although he had not known what to say to her (he never had known what to say) he had been kind and gentle with her; she, in her turn, had willingly given herself to his needs and his service and, as far as she knew, he had never been unfaithful to her. He seldom thanked her for anything, but he had accepted all that she had given and had been strengthened and comforted by it, and that was all the thanks she had wanted. Trust was a stronger link than passion and they had trusted each other for a long time. But in the night he had taken her into his arms, just as she was, sweating, dishevelled, unwashed, and stained with the dirt on the floor, and he had managed to tell her that she was beautiful and that he would rather kill her himself than see her taken by another man; so she knew now that he loved her, and without that love, the future seemed a blank desolation. She could not go on.

'No, Elias,' she cried. 'We must stay with you. Let us either die together or live together. We will start now for the mountains.'

Against the singing of his heart, he tried his honest best to persuade her to leave him. But when he saw that she was steadfastly minded to go with him he shrugged his shoulders, picked up Huda, and they set off together through the mud toward the grey east.

10

They plodded back to the main road by a middle path to
avoid the streams of people pouring into the two towns and
converging on the palace. They crossed the main road a
little south of their own city and they walked barefoot, for
their shoes had stuck fast in the mud. The highway was
sharp with shrapnel, and Sami cut his foot, but he limped
on bravely, for he was, at heart, a soldier, and there was
still, to him, something vaguely glorious about this drama
of war.

They walked on in silence, desperate and exhausted, too
tired to fear much, just concentrating on the next step. Also,
with the coming of daylight, the bombardment had started
again and the guns were cracking to north and south as the
devastation of the two cities continued. They found a path
through the cultivated fields and plodded on toward the
upper road.

'If we can climb a little,' said Elias suddenly, 'and you
can hide in the bushes, I will slip down through the trees
and see if the car is still working. Have we any food?'

They had some sodden biscuits and olives, a few oranges
they had picked up in the groves, a bunch of raw turnips
from the field and plenty of water. The prospect of
breakfast cheered them a little and they crouched under a
pomegranate bush and sucked an orange each. No one had
seen them so far, for it was a grey misty day and the
visibility was poor. Clouds hung low over the mountains
and it looked as though it would soon rain again. They
travelled slowly now, and it was afternoon when they
veered north and crouched in the wood a little way above

their own home. The town lay hidden by a pall of smoke and the noise of destruction and demolition almost deafened them. The car was not far below them, well concealed.

'Be careful, Elias,' said Rosa sharply. She had kept close by his side all day and could not bear to be parted.

'I'll be careful,' said Elias. 'It is only a few hundred yards down the hill. If it is still there and if it still goes, you must come out and meet me on the road in about ten minutes time.'

They finished munching their turnips and trailed out to the road. A single stormy line of sunset hung angrily over the sea. Hordes of people were still hurrying like ants in the direction of the coast and fleets of small boats were still setting out. They stood tense, waiting, straining their ears, and then . . . unbelievably, they heard it. It came round the corner, chugging a little uncertainly, and the relief was so great that they burst out laughing and crying together. But Elias at the wheel was not laughing. He told them to get in quickly and to be careful of broken glass, and they saw that the windscreen and lamps were shattered.

'Hurry,' said Elias. 'It is starting to rain and the roads are dangerous. If the rain beats into our eyes it will be impossible to drive, or without lamps when darkness falls. But we can go a little way, just up to the rocks. There we shall find some shelter.'

Lamia never forgot that ride, for in some ways it was almost as terrifying as the siege. The road wound up in hairpin bends, and by the time they had left the villages behind them it was pouring, and beginning to get dark. The wind whipped the rain into their eyes blinding them, and Elias drew the car off the road.

'It is impossible to go further,' he said flatly, 'but the rocks are near. Come, children, bring the blankets and follow me.'

They slumped in their wet seats, too stiff and weary to move, but their mother encouraged them in a last effort.

'Come,' she said. 'Just one more little climb and there will be shelter. Sami, you shall find us a cave and we will eat the olives and the turnips. Look, Father has his pocket torch and is looking for a place.'

She made it all sound like a game and once again they rose to the occasion and stumbled up the slope. In among the rocks, the sudden cessation of wind and driving rain made it feel quite warm and they found a rough little cave under an overhanging crag.

'We shall sleep dry here,' said Rosa. She huddled the children under the blankets and they fell asleep almost immediately, too tired even to feel hungry, while she and her husband sat watching them for a little while, gnawing turnips. They were cold, wet and exhausted but it was wonderful to sit in safety beyond the noise of gunfire. They suddenly realised how quiet it was.

'It has stopped raining,' said Elias.

'Yes,' said Rosa. 'Look! Lean over, Elias, and look round the wall of the cave.'

He peered round her; the clouds had broken, and a pale moon washed the valley below them with silver. Lower down the mountain it would shine on the slaughter and the dying, but up here, among the rocks, it seemed to be spreading healing and benediction. She leaned up against him and they talked in a sleepy sort of way.

'I'm glad we stayed together,' said Rosa. 'It all turned out for the best.'

'Yes, I'm sorry for those poor people tossing on the sea tonight.'

'And they may never see their men again . . . we were fortunate to get across that main road.'

'The children have been magnificent; no one grumbled or made a fuss.'

'Yes, I am proud of our children; tomorrow, please God, we will get them to safety ... Oh Elias, I'm so glad we stayed together.'

He got up and spread the remaining two blankets, and took her in his arms. She murmured her evening prayer against his shoulder and they both slept.

Rosa woke at daybreak and was relieved to hear no patter of rain. They still had a little food packed away in the car; there were dried figs, olives and some cheese so they could all have some breakfast. It was a quiet, cold dawn with low overcast skies. The children were still asleep.

Elias and Rosa carried Huda and Moomi down to the car and laid them on the seats without waking them. Elias ran back to fetch the last blankets, and Rosa, Lamia and Sami stood serving out their rations on the bonnet. They had already drunk from little pools in the rock and were impatient to be off. In the silence of the hills they heard the other car coming a long way off, but they were not alarmed, for many refugees, like themselves, would be on the road today and some would have sought shelter in the villages behind and would struggle on by daylight.

The jeep came down the road at high speed, heavily armed, with guns sticking through the roof. Ali, the driver, had been engaged in fighting in the mountains and was determined to join his army and be in at the kill when they finally destroyed those Christian vermin on the coast. Up there, in the east of the city, only a week ago, the Christians had bombed and destroyed a Moslem slum area with savage ferocity. Ali ground his teeth at the thought and accelerated to his revenge. He had recruited as many as he could squash into the jeep, amongst them his own fifteen year-old son, Rashid, on his first trip to real warfare.

The boy fingered the trigger of his gun lovingly and shivers of fear and delight ran through him. He had been trained to shoot but he had never yet fired at a live target and he could hardly wait. The jeep rounded a bend in the road fast and suddenly, and there was a car with a smashed windscreen. Two little children were asleep inside and a woman, a girl and a boy, mud-stained and shivering, stood round the bonnet eating their breakfast. Christian vermin, running from their conquerors! The temptation was irresistible; Rashid levelled his gun and, with a shout of triumph, he let fire.

The woman saw him first, just before he pulled the trigger, and leaped in front of the two older children, her arms spread wide like a figure on a crucifix. He riddled her body and the front of the car and leaned out of the window to see her slump to the ground.

'Don't waste your ammunition on women and children,' snapped his father. 'You'll need it for men within an hour's time.' He glanced in the mirror. 'Not a bad shot all the same,' he observed grudgingly.

Rosa was not dead when Elias came leaping down the slope. The trigger-happy young gunner had missed her heart, but the bullets had pierced her lung and lower abdomen and she was bleeding freely internally. He had seen it before, and he knew it could not be long. Her breathing was fast and shallow but she was looking at him he thought, and she was still conscious. Not heeding the screams of his children, he was grovelling in the mud beside her, calling her name, telling her that he loved her, cursing himself because he had never said it before.

It was quite unnecessary, because she had known it all along. She tried to tell him so but it was getting very dark and everything seemed confused and far away . . . Elias . . . Lamia . . . Amin . . . Where was Amin? . . . the Figure on the crucifix and some little children . . . Someone was calling her, telling her that he loved her, but she was not quite sure which one it was; perhaps it was all of them, but

90

at first the voices seemed to be holding her back, and then it was just one, clear, well-known voice calling her forward. 'I know, I know,' she whispered, 'nothing else matters.' Then she closed her eyes because it was time to sleep and she did not speak again. Only Elias crouched beside her on the road and howled like a wild animal in pain.

All her life Lamia could never clearly recall the events of the next hour. They told her later that she fainted, but she could not remember that; she could only see disconnected pictures in vivid colours and sharp detail. There were other people hurrying toward the mountains away from the massacre, most of whom had slept in the village further down, and there was a man who helped Elias take out the tools from the boot of the car and scratch out a shallow grave. She noticed that he was weeping, and heard him say that he too had buried a little daughter who had died of wounds, a mile or so back. She never forgot the whiteness of her mother's face when someone threw the first handful of earth over it, nor the coldness of the stones when they piled them up like a cairn . . . And she remembered other things too; strange things to notice at such a time, like the drifts of wild cyclamen in wet grass round the grave, and the good smell of earth softened by rain. There was the sound of unbroken, hopeless crying, too, the crying of a child who has come to the end of its tether, and after a while she realized that it was Huda, lying on her face among the cyclamen, and Moomi was patting her and trying to comfort her.

There was nothing to do but to go, and at that point they noticed that the radiator of the car had been pierced through and through, and realized that they would have to travel on foot like everyone else. Huda lay limp as a little rag doll, and Elias picked her up and slung her over his shoulder. Lamia tied Moomi on her back with one of the remaining blankets and Sami carried what he could of the remaining food and bedding. They set off into the mist. There was nothing else to do.

The next village was several miles ahead, and Lamia never knew how far she had walked before she suddenly realised that she could go no further. Moomi's sleeping weight was bearing her down and she was sinking to the ground. But just as she fell, someone saw her plight, and lifted Moomi from her back and steadied her. It was the man who had buried his little daughter, and he hoisted Moomi on to his own shoulders in place of the child who had died.

The relief was so great that Lamia began to weep for the first time. She stretched her back and lifted up her head. The mists had rolled back and the cloud had parted, and through the prism of her tears she saw a gleam of sun lighting up the village, not far ahead; and it looked like some celestial city, bathed in the colours of the rainbow.

11

It took them another two days to reach their destination. They rested for a few hours at the first village, but there were hundreds of others and food was scarce, so they trudged on. As they climbed up towards the snows and the cedars, it grew colder, and if they had not had a short lift on a lorry and found a barn in which to sleep, Lamia wondered if they might not all have died too from weariness, cold and hunger, and she half wished that they had.

But when, on the evening of the second day, they trailed down the street of the village where their grandparents lived, the little ones almost forgot their heartbreak in the prospect of rest and food. It was a stormy evening and the sunset tinted the high snows as they climbed the steps of the house where they had spent so many happy summers, and Sami and Huda ran into their grandmother's arms.

'Where is Rosa?' the old woman's eyes asked the question over the children's heads and saw the answer in Elias's face. But there was no time to sit and mourn immediately, for the children had to be fed and washed and comforted before they fell asleep.

They slept and slept, hour after hour, like little creatures that hibernate only waking to eat and drink and sleep again; and while they slept, the clouds lifted and the sun shone out, and they finally woke to the news that Syrian troops had marched in to restore law and order, another peace treaty had been signed, and the war was over. Elias, restless and haggard, strolled up on the track that led to the cedars with Lamia clinging to his arm. There was little place for him in the house, for visitors came all day to mourn with Asea over the death of her daughter, and the little home was packed from morning till night.

'If it is over, I must go back,' said Elias, 'and see what is left of my goods and property. I still have money in the bank and must start business again as soon as possible. You cannot all live here for nothing.'

'Let me come with you, Father.'

'No, it is impossible; we do not know what is left of our home or whether we can live in it again. Besides, who knows whether this peace will hold? Sami and Huda must go to school with the nuns at the convent, and you must study on your own and help your grandmother. It is too much for her to manage alone.'

'I have no books, Father.'

'If the peace holds, I will come back in one of the service cars, and bring you your books.'

'Father, please! Let me and Moomi come with you.'

He looked down at her; she was very like Rosa when she had first come to him and he had never felt deeper love for his daughter than now. It was a bleak prospect to go back to his bombed home alone.

'No,' he said at last, 'you must stay here. The little ones need you. You are their mother now.'

He left two days later in a public car, for the roads were considered relatively safe again, and Lamia found the days intolerably long and purposeless without him. Yet she had to admit that the children needed her. Her grandfather was out in the fields most of the day and her grandmother bowed down with grief and mourning. Besides, Moomi, with the fierce blood of the Commandos in his veins, was not the sort of child Asea had been used to, and she regarded him with suspicion bordering on dislike. He was certainly no child of Rosa's and far be it from her to ask questions, but she did not entirely believe Lamia's account of his origin. If the story was true, why had Lamia been so angry when her grandfather had made the very sensible suggestion of giving him to the nuns? The nuns would have been very good for such a gay, irrepressible, self-willed little piece of quicksilver and would have taught him his place in no time. His peals of laughter, and sparkling black eyes, and the amazing pace with which he propelled himself through life were out of keeping in a house of mourning and, besides, the very sight of him made her feel tired.

Huda settled well. She was her granny's favourite, and although she often sobbed into her pillow at night, she was happy by day, for the nuns were kind and gentle and Huda loved them. But Sami did not settle; he resented being taught by women and his heart ached for his mother. It was only the fear of his grandfather's stick that kept him in class at all, and Lamia could guess where he went after school hours. His grandparents thought he was playing with the village boys but Lamia knew better. One day when he had been absent for hours she went to look for him; she met him at the edge of the village and sniffed at him.

'You've been shooting, Sami,' she said desperately, 'I can smell it. You know how angry Father would be — and anyhow, what's the point, when the war is over? Haven't we lost enough?'

'Who says the war is over?' retorted Sami. 'Have people forgotten the killings and have we forgotten Amin and Mother?'

She stared down at him in silence, for he had never before spoken to her like this, and she had not realized how, in the past weeks, he had grown up. The eager, smooth young face lifted to hers was no longer that of a child, but that of a grave, responsible boy, and he seemed older than his twelve years. She made one more half-hearted attempt to dissuade him.

'But you won't kill the soldier who killed Mother; you'll kill someone else . . . then they will kill someone in revenge who has never done any harm, and so it goes on for ever. Besides, our father . . .'

'If they attack the village, Lamia, they will kill the lot of you, and wouldn't Father wish me to defend you? You've got to help me, Lamia, it's only once a week.'

'And why not?' she thought. If ever she met Kamal or the handsome, laughing lad who had sniped at her mother she knew what she would do to them. She felt closer to this mature child than to any of the others. And besides, she knew perfectly well that she could not stop him, any more than she could stop the wind or the springtime, for this was the very upsurging of his young life.

'What do you want me to do, Sami?' she asked.

'Just to let me out when everyone is asleep, and to let me in again at dawn when I throw gravel up to your window, and wake me again in the morning. There's no school tomorrow, but don't leave me too long or the grandparents will wonder why.'

'All right, Sami,' she promised, and he suddenly smiled up at her with his little boy grin and winked, and they went into the house laughing. The evening passed as usual; grandparents and children went to bed early in the winter time, and, when the house was quiet, Lamia let Sami out and pressed a packet of food into his hand.

'I saved it at supper,' she whispered. 'Goodbye, and God keep you, Sami.'

She locked the door behind him and went to bed, but the thought of him standing, small and weary, somewhere out in the cold under those great blazing stars, kept her awake for a long time. But in the end she must have slept, for she dreamed of a bombardment and woke, sweating, to hear the soft rattle of gravel against her window. She hurried down in the dark to open the door and Sami stumbled into the house, shivering.

'Was it all right, Sami?'

'Yes, but I'm so c-c-cold. Lamia, I want to go to bed, quick.'

She covered him with her blankets as well as his own, and in a few minutes he was breathing deeply. She climbed into bed with Huda, but this time sleep was impossible. For the first time she had looked right beyond her own grief, and the responsibility of the little family weighed heavily on her. 'They will all go,' she thought. 'Amin . . . Mother . . . Father may be bombed . . . Sami may be shot outside the village. Huda will stay here; she loves Granny better than me. There's only Moomi, for sure.'

Moomi! She got up and went to the window that faced north. Day was breaking. If she leaned far out and looked eastwards she could see the sky brightening over the Syrian border, and turning west, she watched the snows catch fire above the cedars. Clear through the cold silence, she seemed to hear her mother's voice, 'If she comes, and can prove that he is hers, I swear by God that we will give him back.'

'Abadan!' breathed Lamia, which is the never, never of eternity. 'It was her oath, not mine.' Suddenly she found she was trembling with fear and anger, for the lull was holding and people were beginning to travel more freely. Any day now, someone might come. They would travel through the cultivated fields at the top of the village, and they would ask questions. A terrible sense of danger hung over her, and a great purpose welled up in her heart. If Sami could guard the village, then she could guard Moomi. She would never let him go. Abadan! Abadan!

From that day on, she patrolled the road to the coast as carefully as any sentry on duty, slipping out a dozen times a day to watch the arrival of cars chugging up from the valleys and lower villages. There was very little traffic, although people were beginning to go back to the towns, and every public car that came up, went down crammed. To his great annoyance, she refused to allow Moomi to walk to the top of the village, where fascinating little paths led up to the snow and the cedars. She kept him a prisoner and made him play under the fig tree in her grandparents' garden, and he did not like it at all. He was growing strong and wilful, and she often wondered how long they could go on living like this.

It came to an end quite soon; it was a clear spring day. Sami and Huda were at school, and Moomi bolted safely into his enclosure. Lamia slipped out of the house while her grandmother's back was turned and hurried up the street to where the mountain road came twisting down a little way to meet the village. A car was arriving; it stopped to put down a passenger, and then speeded on to the Square, and Lamia stood completely still, for she knew who this passenger was and this was exactly what she had expected to see.

A middle-aged woman in the black headdress of a Palestinian stood, irresolute by the side of the road, afraid to enter a Christian village. Lonely, but dignified, she advanced slowly, holding her head proudly, with the courage born of great love, and Lamia walked to meet her for, whatever happened, she must not let her reach the village or ask questions. Where Moomi was concerned, it was a case of once seen never forgotten, and he was already distressingly well-known and popular.

'Can I help you?' Lamia spoke quietly and pleasantly, choking back the unreasonable tide of hate and fear that seemed to be welling up inside her. More than guns or bombardments, this tired queenly woman threatened her very life and was therefore her mortal enemy.

The woman lifted her hands to heaven and murmured a

prayer; then she made a courteous little gesture of beseeching.

'I have come for my daughter's child,' she said. 'They say he was found and brought up here by those who fled the massacre on the coast . . . Oh my daughter, help me! I am afraid to enter the village. Go and bring me news. He is a beautiful child and his mother was killed in the month of May, in the orange groves above the camp. She went out to try and speak with her husband . . . my only daughter . . . they found her body; but the child had gone.'

Lamia thought fast. It was important to find out all she could about her adversary.

'Where is his father?' she asked.

'He was wounded on black Saturday,' replied the woman quietly. 'My sons are all fighting. He is all I have. By the mercy of God, my daughter, go and ask!'

'There are many children in the village, and many have fled from the massacre. How shall I know him?'

'When his mother was pregnant, someone looked upon him with an evil eye. The child has a great purple mark on his back; besides, I have this.'

She opened her shopping bag, drew out a leather case containing a little money and a photograph of a Commando in battle dress with his arm round his wife and baby boy. It was about two years old, but there was no mistaking Moomi. He was straining forward towards the camera, black eyes flashing, wilful and merry. Lamia looked at it a long time and shuddered because the girl had been young and beautiful and alive; quite unlike the huddled creature that had sprawled on the earth under the orange tree.

'I know that child' she said at last. 'He came to the village; but they are not here now. When peace was declared they went back to their home. The woman who cared for him was shot in the road by your people and I heard the father say that he would give the child to the nuns.'

'Gone?' the woman breathed the word like a desolate cry and all the grief of the world seemed embodied in it. For a moment Lamia thought the trembling figure would fall, but she did not stretch out her hand to support her.

'Gone where?' repeated the woman. 'Oh my daughter, may God have mercy on you, but tell me where they have gone.'

'I do not know; probably back to their home on the coast, but if I hear of them I will send you word. Have you an address?'

Tears were coursing down the woman's cheeks, but she fished in her bag again and brought out a piece of paper with a telephone number on it. 'There's a grocer's shop at the entrance of the camp,' she whispered, 'and I have a room above it. If you should ring that number and ask for Oom Aisha, they will call me.'

She hesitated, and advanced a few steps, clasping her hands.

'Is there no one else in the village who could give me news? Had these people no relatives?'

'I am their relative; I will let them know. You must not come into the village. Many there have suffered at the hands of your people and they might harm you. You had better go back to the main road and wait for a car.'

'Of your goodness . . . a drink of water.' She was still courteous and dignified but her strength seemed exhausted.

'There is a spring up there on the hillside,' said Lamia turning away. 'You had better go. There are fierce dogs in the village and they might set them loose on you.'

She did not look at her again, but stood staring at the houses below them, hoping a car would come soon and that no one else would appear. She walked slowly toward the village and, only when she reached the first straggling houses, did she turn her head. The woman was stumbling blindly up the hill toward the spring. 'She looks as though she would fall,' thought Lamia, 'and she has nothing with which to draw water.' But she did not care; an enemy is an enemy in war time, and they had not cared at all when Amin and her mother fell.

The hired car was roaring up the street. There was room for one more passenger and they would pick up the woman and take her away for ever. The incident had been entirely successful and she even knew what district to avoid when people began to move about freely again. She reached her grandparents' house and there was Moomi, kicking angrily at the gate of his cage and shouting for liberty.

She pulled back the bolt, caught him up in her arms and hugged him passionately. He kicked her and struggled to be free so she set him down and he stuck out his tongue at her, laughed and started running, for this was what he had longed for; to run where he liked, with the whole wide world and the mountains ahead of him. Lamia ran beside him, up the village street, and out into the sweet wildness of early spring, where all the fear had gone. Moomi jumped and rolled in the grass like a clumsy baby goat and she tossed him up in the air and laughed with him. He was safe and here for ever; no one would ever take him away from her now.

'Abadan,' she muttered. 'Abadan!'

Only she wished she could forget the clenched hands, the trembling lips, and the extreme pallor of the woman's face.

12

Yes, it was good to be free of that haunting fear, to relax her watchfulness, and to know that Moomi was safe, but it was not quite the relief she had expected, for something else had taken the place of her fear; something harder to cope with, because she could do nothing about it, and that was a feeling of guilt. However much she tried, she could not forget that Moomi was now stolen property, not really hers at all, and, worse still, she had broken her mother's vow. Instead of being happier, she became more depressed, more impatient with the older children, more restless and frustrated. Her grandmother longed to comfort her, but Lamia was shut into herself. She helped mechanically in the house, but wandered out on to the hillside as soon as her tasks were finished, or withdrew into a corner of the room. Only with Moomi was she always gentle, watching him awake, brooding over him asleep. His merry laughter was the only sound that brought a smile to her face, and her grandparents said no more about giving him to the nuns.

It was a relief when her father came up for the night about the middle of February and brought her school books. It was a cold wet day and they sat in the house, sipping coffee and talking, while her grandmother prepared a festal meal. The younger children were still at school.

'What's the house like, Father?' asked Lamia.

'Not as bad as I expected. The back windows are broken and the walls and furniture in the back room pitted with bullets, but the front of the house is all right, praise be to God.'

'Have you started business again, Father?'

'Oh yes, in a small way. I've rented a room in the district, as I have no car. I had bales of material hidden under the floorboards and I am doing quite well. People are beginning to walk freely in the streets now and to buy and sell.'

'And we have not been looted?'

'No, praise God. Georges guarded the house well with the help of two fierce dogs. I think no Moslem dares to come so far inside a Christian quarter. Besides, the Syrians are coming down hard on looters. They shot ten of them the other day.'

'But why should they govern our country?'

He shrugged. 'They are probably the only people who can protect our position. They have drawn up a new programme of reform, and the President is still a Maronite.'

'Father, do you think the peace will hold?'

His face suddenly looked old and weary. He shrugged his shoulders again.

'They were discussing it on the radio last night. They say the reforms don't measure up to the sacrifices that have been made — maybe 40,000 deaths, one in five buildings destroyed, half the factories burned or looted, and neither side has achieved what it wanted. Some are hopeful, but I think the bitterness will not die in a hurry. There are many ready to fight on.'

'Father, let me come home; me and Moomi. I hate to think of you alone in the house.'

He looked at her thoughtfully. It would be good to have her there. He did not try to tell her what it felt like coming home in the evening to the spoiled house, cooking his own unappetising supper, dreading the loneliness of the nights. Schools were beginning to re-open and things were quiet at present.

'I think you could come back at the end of the month,'

he said slowly. 'Huda should stay till Easter and finish the term.' Then he asked abruptly, 'What is Sami doing? I suppose he has joined the local defence group?'

She nodded. 'I couldn't stop him, Father; all the boys are in it. Besides, it keeps him happy and helps him to forget. He loves his gun.'

'How often does he go out?'

'Only once a week.'

'Do the grandparents know?'

'No. I let him out when they are asleep, and let him in before they wake. I'm sorry, Father, but what else could I do?'

'Nothing; he's lost too much. He's like all the others. No one will rest until their own personal loss is avenged. This war will not end yet. But if you come, Sami should stay here; I suppose he's learning something at the convent, and he will get into more serious trouble in the city.'

'And Moomi, Father? He must come. The grandparents could never cope with him alone.'

'Yes, Moomi come too.' He was sitting on the floor, quiet for once, playing with a little car that Elias had brought him, and they had forgotten about him. 'Moomi come too,' he repeated, 'in his car,' and he rubbed his curls against Elias's trouser leg.

'How can you get on with your schooling if you have to attend to Moomi?'

'We must find a woman to look after the house, Father, and she can take care of Moomi while I'm at school. There must be thousands homeless. It should not be difficult.'

He shrugged again. 'No, it should not be difficult. Most of the houses to the west of us are destroyed. Hanni's house has a great hole through the wall.'

Hanni! She had barely thought of him since her mother's death. It was strange how life now seemed to fall into separate compartments: life before Amin died, life before

Moomi came, life before her mother died. They had all changed since then, but Hanni would not have changed. He belonged to the old, happy days of their childhood and the anguished days of Amin's murder. She had left him bitter and hurt and had longed to comfort him. Perhaps now they could comfort each other.

'Is Hanni all right?' she asked eagerly. 'I should like to see Hanni again. Do you think he would come and fetch us down?'

'He's on sick leave at the moment. There was a gun fight in the hospital and a bullet pierced his wrist. His arm is in plaster but he went on working and treating wounds until things eased off. If he was free, he would like to visit you. He has asked me about you each time I have met him.' Elias glanced at his daughter and her cheeks flushed, but they said no more because, at that moment, the children arrived home from school. Instead of their usual restrained greeting, they both flung themselves into their father's arms. Huda clung to him tightly and began to cry as though her heart would break.

Lamia watched them moodily. She had not realised that their young hearts were so hungry and, wrapped up in her own private problems, she had not helped them much. Her nagging sense of failure deepened. 'If I go away,' she thought, 'they will hardly miss me. They are as lonely with me as they will be without me. Oh, Mother, Mother! Everything has gone wrong! We aren't a family any more.'

Her father left next day while the children were in school. She and Moomi walked to the public car with him, and Moomi made a scene, because he wanted to squash in on top of all the others and had to be held back. She watched the car drive off through a blur of tears and she was not weeping for her father, because she would soon go to him. She wept because of her kind old grandparents with whom she had never really managed to communicate;

because of Sami and Huda, who no longer turned to her for help; because of her mother's oath, which lay heavy on her conscience. She turned back to the house sick at heart although the sun was shining and the grass a shimmering green after yesterday's rain. As she reached the top of the village street, a child came running to meet her.

'Lamia, a man is asking for you in the market place. They are taking him to your house. I came to tell you.'

A man! Had that terrible smoke-stained devil come himself to claim Moomi? If so, it was no use running away. Her only hope was to reach the house first and lock him into the enclosure. She picked him up and ran furiously down the road. He yelled and struggled but she took no notice and she reached the steps just as a little crowd of children, escorting the stranger, turned the corner from the market place. 'There she is,' she heard one of them say as she flung Moomi headlong through the garden gate and bolted it behind her; and, even as she did so, she realised that concealment was impossible, because the child's screams were enough to rouse the village, and she knew him well enough to know that he would not stop until he got what he wanted.

Very well, then! She would fight for him. She clenched her fists and marched towards the little procession. Flinging back her head she stared into the new-comer's face, her eyes dark with hate, and then gave a little sobbing cry and swayed on her feet. Hanni stepped forward and held her by the arm.

'Lamia,' he cried, and his voice was warm and loving, 'are you all right? Come back to the house, my dear, and sit down. Lean on my arm.'

She was deathly white and trembling, and for a moment Hanni thought she was going to faint. But the excited clamour of the children jerked her to her senses, and the colour flooded back into her cheeks. 'I . . . I'm all right,' she said. 'I . . . I . . . just thought you were someone else. Come into the house.'

She released Moomi, who burst out of the enclosure roaring, with a running nose and a crimson face. His feelings were badly hurt, for Lamia had never before flung him roughly on the ground and slammed the door on him, and he simply could not understand it. He retired into a corner and sat for a long time, hiccoughing and sniffing, and refused to be comforted.

Lamia sank down into a chair and gave a shaky little smile. 'I'm sorry,' she said. 'I thought you were someone else.'

'Who? "Someone else" had a queer effect on you! Were you disappointed it was only me?'

'Oh no! I was glad, so glad. I thought it was someone coming to take Moomi away. Oh Hanni, my father has just left and I sent you a message.'

'Did you? I did not know that he was coming up, or I'd have sent you a message.' His face became grave. 'I wanted to come and tell you how sad I was about your mother.'

Grandmother came in at that moment and was delighted to see a young man, and bustled round preparing coffee and cakes. She did not approve of advanced education for girls and considered that it was high time for Lamia to be thinking about matrimony, as her own daughter had done at sixteen; — only in those days it was the parents who thought of matrimony and the daughter did as she was told. Times had changed, she thought sadly. Nevertheless, this was a fine upstanding young man with good manners and an honest face, and the girl could do a lot worse for herself.

Lamia poured the coffee and gathered Moomi into her lap. He gave an immense sigh, curled himself into a ball and fell asleep instantly, as though the problems of life were just too much for him. She and Hanni chatted politely as they drank, and then Hanni stood up. 'Put Moomi on the bed and tell your granny we are going for a walk,' he said. 'We can't talk here. Let's climb up to the snows.'

They walked demurely up the street, but once outside the village he took her hand and they climbed together. She looked about her as one whose eyes had been opened, seeing for the first time that spring had come early to the mountain, noticing things she had never noticed before — the first sprays of almond blossom in the terraced gardens around the village, the green of springing grass, the purple drifts of cyclamen in the hollows. They climbed till the grass turned yellow, because the snow had just melted and runnelled into streams, and meadow saffrons and stars of Bethlehem flowered at the edge of the drifts. They found a rock and sat down, warm and glowing and out of breath, and turned to the great mountainous landscape, for the sunlight on the snow was dazzling and they could not look at it. And here, for the first time since her mother's death, Lamia really talked, pouring out her grief, her failure to take her mother's place, her fears for Sami and Moomi, her determination to keep what was no longer hers, and Hanni listened without once interrupting. Down in the hospital he had often watched a surgeon lance a deep abcess that had formed round a shrapnel wound, and seen the poison pour out unchecked, knowing that, afterwards, the fever would abate and the patient would sleep in peace. So he sat watching the girl he was just beginning to love, knowing that if she could pour out all the horror of the past weeks, she too would find peace.

She talked until the sun had sunk toward the western ridge, bathing the hills and high snows and valleys in that golden afternoon light that illumines every detail. When she had finished she turned to him like a tired child coming home.

'So what shall I do?' she asked. 'And how shall we ever all start again?'

He sat silent, because he had something to tell her and did not know how to begin. She glanced up at him, saw the quietness in his eyes and the half-smile on his face and unconsciously gave him the help he needed.

'And you, Hanni?' she asked. 'When I last saw you, you were miserable; now you are different. What has happened? I suppose things are better at the hospital, now that the war is over.'

He shook his head slowly. 'I don't think the war is over. Casualties still come in every day. It's horrible . . . and, by the way, Lamia, Kamal was brought in a week or two ago. A bomb had burst quite close to him. His face was all blasted and they had to amputate his arm, so you've had your revenge.'

'Kamal!' She stiffened and her eyes flashed angrily. 'Tell me, what did you do? I wish you had killed him.'

'He'd probably have been grateful if I had. What boy of seventeen wants to live maimed and looking like that? However, I didn't; I helped carry him up to the ward. He was conscious when he came in and we talked a little. He knew me.'

Lamia's face was contorted with anger. 'You . . . you *talked* to him?'

'Yes . . . I forgave him . . . because you see . . . I've been forgiven.'

He spoke so quietly that she could only just hear him, and she wondered if she had heard aright.

'You, forgiven?' she spluttered. 'Whatever have *you* done to deserve forgiveness? Whereas *he* . . . Oh Hanni, how *could* you?'

She turned away from him; her sudden spurt of anger had left her feeling weak and hopeless, but Hanni was talking, rather uncertainly, as though groping for words and she had to listen, whether she wanted to or not.

'I was almost as much to blame for Amin's death as Kamal was,' he said steadily, 'and I almost went mad after he died. I knew Kamal was dangerous; I was nearly two years older than Amin and I could have persuaded him . . . If I had tried hard enough and kept my temper, he would have listened to me. But he told me I was a coward and I was angry . . . I was too proud to try again. I watched him walk to his death through the orange trees and I did not go after him!'

He waited, but Lamia's face was still turned away. She did not speak or move.

'After he died, I think it was like being in hell . . . Guilt is a terrible thing, Lamia. You wake in the night and the stars are no longer beautiful. You walk on the hills and the first flowers are no longer lovely. All the colour goes out of life. It is like a great burden . . . your heart is always heavy, until you feel that it will crush you.'

'You don't look particularly crushed now,' said Lamia coldly.

'No, that's what I am trying to tell you. There came a night when I had been dealing with horrors all day, and at night the bombardment was so fierce that we, who were off duty, went down into a shelter under a big block of flats. I think it was a big underground garage. As I sat there, I suddenly decided to end it all, to run out into the middle of the guns and to go wherever Amin had gone . . . only there was this terrible burden, and I supposed there was a God somewhere. I sat sweating and trembling because I couldn't face life and I couldn't face death.'

'Well, you seem to have got over it now,' persisted Lamia.

'That's what I'm trying to tell you; there was a man in the shelter that night. Everyone else was tense and terrified, but he did not seem to be afraid. He gathered the children round him and played a guitar and taught them little songs – songs about the love of God. Then he turned to us and we, too, gathered round him. He told us that his wife and children had left for the States that day – his wife was an American but he had stayed because he had a message for us.'

'From whom? Was he a political leader?'

'No . . . a message from God. Between the blasts, he spoke about the cross.'

'That old crucifix? It didn't help Mother much, did it? I think I'm an atheist, Hanni.'

'I think I was, too. But he didn't speak about Someone who had died centuries ago, but Someone whose death is always powerful – today as much as ever. He knew we were all thinking about death in any case, and he told us to think about that one death that can take the sting out of every other death. He somehow talked as though Christ had died that same day . . . for me, for all the sins I had committed, all the wrong things I had done.'

'So what?' Lamia had turned and was watching him curiously.

'He said there was only one really important question when we have to face death – where is my sin? Am I carrying it myself, as a heavy burden that will separate me from God for ever . . . or have I laid it on Christ on the cross? If so, then death is the gate of life. He read to us from the Bible.'

'A Bible? Was he a priest then?'

'No, he wasn't a priest. He had been in hotel management. We talked together when we could hear ourselves speak, and I told him what I had wanted to do and why. About two o'clock in the morning there was a lull. People slept all round us, but he read to me from his Bible by the light of a torch. Listen, Lamia, this is what he read.'

He drew a small Bible from the pocket of his jacket and turned the pages slowly. It was very quiet up there on the border of the snow, and the whole mountain and sky seemed to be listening.

"But because of our sins he was wounded, beaten because of the evil we did. We are healed by the punishment he suffered, made whole by the blows he received. All of us were like sheep that were lost, each of us going his own way. But the Lord made the punishment fall on him . . ."

'And then?'

'Well, it was as though my load was lifted; laid on Somebody else. I wanted to live, not die. I knew I was forgiven.'

'So you don't care any more? You'll just sit down and forgive? And do nothing more about Amin and Mother? You'll let them win, hands down?'

'No . . .' he was struggling to explain, pleading with her to understand. 'No, it's not like that. You see, we always prayed to a dead man on a crucifix, but we'd got it all wrong. Christ is *alive* . . . He takes the burden, and then he comes to us, and then everything starts afresh. It's like being born again. We forgive because we have been forgiven, and we love because we have been loved. Lamia, did anyone ever conquer hate with hate, or darkness with deeper darkness, or evil with more evil? If you worked in that hospital, you'd know. Hate piles on hate and wars never really stop.'

Lamia was shaken in spite of herself.

'But this is a holy war,' she said uncertainly. 'It is right to defend your religion. Don't our soldiers stick crucifixes and pictures of the Virgin on their tanks?'

'Yes, and I expect the boy who shot your mother had a Moslem crescent and a Koran on his jeep. But the cross is God's great sign of love and forgiveness. I think we have

112

got it all wrong, and we have set up our own gods.'

The sun was dipping behind the mountains and the cedars massed black in the shadows. Hanni rose to his feet. 'Come,' he said, 'you had better be in by curfew time. I shall go to the inn and leave by the first car tomorrow morning. I have to be back in hospital by noon.'

They ran down the path towards the village. The first star hung over the convent belfry as they reached the grand parents' front door. Lamia hesitated.

'Won't you come in?' she said.

'No; the house is already overfull and they would not know where to put me. Besides, I was up all last night and I'm going to sleep early.'

He drew the Bible from his pocket. 'Keep it, Lamia,' he said, 'and read the passages I've marked. And come soon!'

He turned away and she watched his straight young figure disappear into the dusk, but she did not go in at once. It was cold in the evening but a south wind was blowing, soft with the scent of earth and growth. Her eyes filled with sudden tears. He was eighteen and she was sixteen and it was spring; yet they had spent most of the afternoon, as far as she could remember, talking about death and guilt. How old, and dull, and weary war made you! They should have laughed and danced and loved, only she wasn't sure whether she loved him or not. She only knew that he was different from any other young person she had ever known.

And yet, she had to admit, Hanni had not really seemed old or dull. In fact, his gladness had irritated her.

Yet now that the gladness had gone, she felt cold and alone.

She could not understand it.

13

The soft patter of gravel against Lamia's window woke her
from a complicated dream, and, at first, she could not
remember what she was meant to do. It was still so dark
and the stars blazed so fiercely above the black mountain
skyline. Then it came back slowly; Sami had gone out on
guard, but what on earth was he doing, coming home in the
middle of the night? She jumped out of bed, drew her
dressing gown round her and fumbled her way to the front
door, and Sami seemed to fall inside with a blast of cold air.

'Sami,' she whispered, 'what is the matter? And why
have you come home in your battle dress? And why in the
middle of the night?'

He stood rigid for a moment and then fell into her arms,
stifling back his sobs, clinging to her.

'Sami, stop! Grandpa will hear. Come into my room and
tell me what happened.' She pushed him into her own bed
where he could bury his face in the pillow and she sat on
the bed holding him and comforting him, as she would
have done a little boy; after all, he is only twelve, she
thought suddenly. It's only war that turns him into a man
at twelve. And gradually he stopped shuddering and rolled
over on his back, and she was able to extract the story, bit
by bit.

'It's Farid, Lamia,' he whispered, 'I think he may be
dead. He lay on the ground, screaming and screaming.'

'Farid? He's younger than you. Whatever happened?'

His answer was punctuated by sniffs and hiccoughs.

'It was so cold . . . we began to run up and down, he at
his post and I at mine; then we met in the village and we

114

began to play a little, pointing our guns at each other. Then suddenly one of the village dogs came running out barking, and gave us a fright. I suppose he pressed the trigger, and the gun went off, but not forward, or it would have killed me. It sort of backfired, up into the air, into his face and he fell on the ground, screaming . . . and he went on screaming and covering his face with his arms and I could not see . . . '

'But where is he now?'

'The others heard him and came; then they fetched his father and he came and carried him home. He was still screaming. He said he couldn't see. Lamia, do you think he's blind?'

'I don't know; and, in any case, it wasn't your fault, Sami. I'll go and get you a hot drink, and stay beside you till you fall asleep. Then I'll go up to Farid's house and find out.'

She crept into the kitchen and heated him a cup of goat's milk. He drank it greedily, flung his arms above his head, and went to sleep almost immediately. Lamia sat beside him for quite a long time, looking down into his flushed tear-stained face and feeling strangely at peace, because this was what her mother would have done. For the first time since her mother's death, she was taking her place, providing some sort of a refuge for these children in the bitter world of war. Later she crept into Sami's bed in a corner of the living room and slept too.

But not for long, for grandfather went out early to his fields, and she woke soon after sunrise. She dressed quickly, glanced at Sami, and let herself out into the glittering world of shining mist and dewdrops. She ran up the empty street and knocked softly at the door of Farid's home. His mother, her dark eyes enormous in her white face, opened it almost at once.

'What is it?' she asked abruptly, and her hand flew to her mouth.

'I just came to ask . . . how is Farid? My brother saw the accident.'

The woman relaxed a little.

'Yes; they were playing together with their cursed guns. What has come to us, that we give guns to children? Come in.'

It was a poor little house, and the younger children were still asleep on mattresses in the inner room. Lamia sat down and waited and after a few moments the woman spoke in a toneless voice.

'His father has taken him to hospital. The military came with a car . . . they think he is blinded . . . my eldest son! How shall we all live? And what will he do? A blind boy!'

'I'm sorry,' murmured Lamia, and rose to go because there was no more to say. The sunlight, springing above the eastern heights and scattering the mists, was almost dazzling as she stepped outside, and she wondered what it would feel like to be blind and never to see the light of the morning again. She suddenly remembered, with a throb of satisfaction, that Kamal might be blind.

Hanni! . . . her tired thoughts strayed, for she had slept very little. Perhaps it was just the beauty of the morning, but the memory of him came like a thought of renewal; his joy seemed to stretch out to her across the troubled miles; 'Everything starts afresh. It's like being born again . . . come back soon, Lamia.'

She knew she must not linger, for there was Moomi to dress and jobs to be done and an explanation to be made as to why she and Sami had slept in each other's beds and why Sami was still asleep. But it suddenly struck her that further concealment was impossible, for everyone would visit Farid's mother in her misfortune and within an hour or two the story would be all over the village. She only hoped her grandfather would not beat poor Sami. He'd had enough!

So she walked in and told her grandparents exactly what had happened, and, though Granny mourned and lamented, the old man gave no sign of surprise. He nodded his bald head and his bright old eyes twinkled.

'Twelve years old!' he muttered, 'And he guards the village! Rosa would be proud of her son.' There was unconcealed pride in his voice.

Lamia was not at all sure that Rosa would be anything of the sort, but it was a relief to have it all out in the open. She watched her grandfather out of the corner of her eye, stealing upstairs to peep at his hero grandson, who slept and slept. The convent bell tolled for school and Granny went to market; the children came out and shouted in the playground, and still Sami slept. Granny, as a great concession, had taken Moomi with her so that the house would be quiet, and Lamia took a pile of the children's mending and went and sat beside her brother. But her hands soon fell idle and she went back to the interrupted current of her thoughts. 'It's like a new beginning; like being born again . . . come back soon, Lamia.'

What did he mean? How could you start again out of this holocaust of death and misery? She stared out of the window to where the village sloped toward the valley; to where, in the terraced gardens, green shoots were already sprouting, and the first green ears were pushing out from the dead grey-ash of the fig tree. The earth was rich and black with humus and compost, and no one had cleared away the rot and decay of winter, for it was the very soil from which the new life drew its riches. You always seemed to come round to death again in the end, the end of life and the birthplace of life. Hanni had said something like that. 'Death is the gate of life.' She knew vaguely that it meant something important, but her thoughts were confused and disconnected and she could not make any sense out of them.

Then she remembered the Bible that Hanni had left her.

She had never read the Bible before because Bibles were mostly in the hands of the priests, who doled out what was suitable to the congregation, but Sami still breathed deeply, the house was quite quiet, and the mending not urgent. She tiptoed to the cupboard and pulled out her Bible from underneath the neglected school books, for she had not yet settled down to study. There was always so much to do in the village, and besides, she found she could not concentrate.

She sat down and found the place that Hanni had marked and the strange words absorbed her. The sun streamed in through the eastern window and rested in healing warmth on her bowed head, but she did not notice. "But he endured the suffering that should have been ours ... we are healed by the punishment he suffered, made whole by the blows he received. All of us were like sheep that were lost, each of us going his own way. But the Lord made the punishment fall on him ..." And as she read she was no longer on the mountain, but down on that desolate road at dawn standing by the car under an overcast sky. The handsome boy with the laughing face cocked his gun, and she knew she was going to die; but she did not die, because her mother stepped in front of her with her arms outstretched and died instead; and that was why she was alive now.

Then, in memory, she was struggling on in the rain, sinking down under Moomi's weight, her feet slipping in the mud. But suddenly the weight was lifted; a man had taken Moomi on to his own back, and she had stood up, lifted her head, and seen the shining rainbow city not far along the road. She had never even thanked the man because he had disappeared in the crowd but, because of him, she had reached the city. She stared at Grandmother's little crucifix on the wall, and knew that, somehow, that death was the source of her life and that figure was bowed beneath her burdens, so that she might travel on free.

'I don't think I'm an atheist any longer,' she thought rather vaguely, but she had no idea what to do about it. She had had a disturbed night and was in no mood for profound thought, yet, as she sat there, she knew she was not alone. The love that had suffered, and died and triumphed over death was round about her, lifting her load, active and watching over her, just as she was watching over her troubled young brother, longing to guard him from evil, planning his welfare.

Before, there had been no future; they were all just at a standstill. Now, perhaps, they were going somewhere. She sat up straight and gazed through the sparkling blue window where the sun poured in. Perhaps they were all moving on, through the storm, toward the rainbow and the shining city. She laid her head on Sami's pillow and dozed very peacefully, until Moomi, fed up with all this unusual quietness, escaped from his grandmother's clutches, and came mooing up the stairs, like the cows he had seen in the market, and woke them both up.

The day passed uneventfully. She and Sami went up, after lunch, to join the crowd of visitors in Farid's house, and Sami, having been on the spot, found himself the centre of attention, although whether the hero of the day or the villain of the piece, Lamia was not quite sure. Farid's father had not yet returned, but he had sent a message that the boy was permanently blinded and his mother sat in hopeless despair, paying little heed to the sympathetic clucking and chattering all round her. Sami answered all the questions steadily enough but when, just before sunset, they started home again, he suddenly burst into tears and was sick in the gutter. Lamia stood, holding his forehead until he had finished and, once again, she recognised this strange new sense of direction. She spoke with certainty.

'Don't worry, Sami,' she said, 'You're not going out

again – at least, not till you're much older. We're going home. Everyone says things are quieter now, and you ought to be in a proper boys' school. I'm going to phone Father tonight, if I can get through.'

Sami looked up at her gratefully. His face was greeny-yellow, his nose was running, and in his eyes was that lost, scared look she had seen in Amin's eyes the day he had come home from the shootings outside the church. She put her arm round his shoulders and led him back to the house, where he sat huddled by the fire until supper time.

Lamia went down to the call-box but the destruction in the city was such that it was still impossible to get through, so there was nothing to do but to try and send messages and wait. It was dark, but a sickle moon hung over the peaks, and she walked slowly for, since morning, she had not again been alone with this new sense of enfolding, wooing, guiding love. It seemed to call for some response and yet she still did not know how to respond or what to do. Tomorrow she would try and find out; she would go to the priest for confession and on Sunday she would go to mass with Grandmother, and she would go on reading Hanni's Bible, although it all looked very difficult and obscure. She began to make a mental list of what she ought to confess, and quickly decided not to go at all because she only knew of one real sin, and that was one she had no intention of confessing; she was far too afraid of what the priest might say about it.

So, in the waiting days, she took her Bible out on the hillside and read the story of Jesus and his love and felt her broken heart warmed – comforted, but not challenged. The glorious weather held and, at the end of the village, flowers bloomed, streams overflowed their runnels, and baby lambs were born. Yet the snows above the cedars still clung to the peaks, and would do so until late spring, in spite of the patient sun warming them day after day. But their time would come; one day spring would prevail, the ice would crack and the melted snow cascade down in great drifts and flood-streams. But not yet . . . not yet.

14

Elias came up to the village at the weekend in slightly
better spirits. The twenty-sixth cease-fire seemed to be
holding and the new Lebanese National Covenant, heavily
backed by Syria, gave rise to hopes for a peaceful settle-
ment. Banks had re-opened, traffic jams were once more
the order of the day, and the airport was functioning.
Stinking garbage had begun to disappear from the streets,
broken glass and twisted metal were being picked up, and
even the mail delivery had re-commenced, bringing letters
posted months before. Schools had re-opened, said Elias
optimistically, and Lamia and Moomi should go back with
him; and when he heard of Sami's latest escapade, he
agreed to take him too.

Lamia thought that she would be glad to leave the
village, but, to her surprise, she found it a sad parting; not
because of what she was leaving, but because of what had
never been. Her staid, old-fashioned grandparents had
sheltered them in their hour of need and she truly loved
them, but she had never been able to show it or communicate, and now that she longed to fling her arms round
her granny's neck, she found that she could not do so. And
then there was Huda; she had not known how much she
loved funny little gap-toothed Huda, with her enormous
eyes and spindly legs. But Huda hardly bothered to say
goodbye to her older sister because she was going to market
with Granny and she was picking out the biggest basket.

It was early morning, and to Lamia's surprise her father
by-passed the road that ran eastward to their old home, and

turned south on the road by which they had arrived. She thought that his grief had made him absent-minded and laid her hand on his knee.

'Father,' she said, 'we can't go this way. The Moslems are still holding the coast.'

'I know, my daughter,' he replied. 'We shall just drive part of the way and turn back.' Then she knew where he was going, and said no more.

She was sad to leave the mountain, too. It was a clear spring day and Lamia gazed moodily out of the car window at the brilliant pastures, the sprays of almond blossom flung against the blue sky, the bright young shoots in the terraced gardens. This strange new sense of being loved was stirring the very roots of her being, as the sun stirred the roots in the frozen ground. Deep within her, love was begetting love. She was beginning to care and notice, but she could not break the barriers and let love go free and so it hurt and constricted. Does loving always hurt like this, she wondered? And if so, is it worth it? Isn't it better to stay hard and frozen and unfeeling? But that is not how the spring comes, nor birth, nor new life . . . Her thoughts were interrupted by Moomi, pulling her nose to make her look at some baby lambs; only her father sat tense and silent at the wheel. Even at that moment they were driving through the streets of the rainbow city which was only a village after all, and shortly after they drew up by the side of the road with the rocks rising to their right and the ravine on the left. Elias dismounted, without a word, and walked to the cairn and none of the children dared to follow him. They sat in the car and watched, and even Moomi fell silent.

Lamia hardly remembered the place for they had arrived in the dark and the shock of the events had driven every other impression away but, in any case, it looked quite different. Her father had been there twice to build up on the cairn and erect a wooden cross, and the rocks round were no longer stark and black; they were clothed with green and the grass was starred with flowers. In the place where she had died there was a garden now, and once again the girl felt that stirring at the frozen roots; love, sorrow and bitter regrets. How completely she had taken her mother for granted and how wilful she had often been! 'Mother, Mother,' she cried in thought, 'if you came back how different it would all be; I'd do anything you wanted.'

Memories flooded back; she was sitting on the floor with her head on her mother's lap, just after Amin's death. 'There is so much more to know,' Rosa had said. 'You will read and travel and find out. But I know one thing; Jesus died because he loved.' Yet she had been wrong in one respect; she, Lamia, with all her education had not known. It was Rosa with her little learning and country wisdom, who had known the ultimate. There had been another evening, too. They had sat in the kitchen and Lamia had stormed, while her mother had cut up a cabbage and talked. 'Faith is kept alive in a heart that loves and forgives.' . . . Loving . . . forgiving . . . that was how Rosa had lived and that was how she had died, whispering that nothing else mattered.

Her father returned, his face a sealed mask, started up the car, backed and turned and Lamia, with a last glance at the grave, suddenly realised that, in those past few moments, the handsome boy with the mocking face and the cocked gun hadn't been there at all. That face, that had haunted her for weeks, had disappeared; only her mother remained with her arms outstretched, dying so that her children could live. Perhaps, she thought rather confusedly, that was what love did; it blotted out the evil and made plain all that belonged to its own realm. Perhaps her mother was right; perhaps nothing else mattered.

Lamia was relieved to find the old home less damaged than she had feared for it had been well protected by the great blocks of flats, many of them now partly destroyed or burnt out. They set out together, as a family, on this new, dreary business of living without their mother, and the glory of spring and the blossom in the neglected garden helped them. Lamia and Sami settled down to their studies until the schools should open. A depressed elderly woman from the suburb, whose house had been destroyed and whose married children had taken their families to Cyprus, moved in to housekeep and look after Moomi. But Moomi's twinkling feet and fertile brain proved too much for her and she was quite unable to control him. He seemed to grow more mischievous and resourceful every day until Lamia almost dreaded leaving the house for fear of what she might hear on her return.

It came to a head one evening when she arrived back to find old Lela sitting weeping, with her apron flung over her head, and Moomi sitting, uncertain and tearful beside the ruins of Huda's little cuckoo clock. He tried to explain that he had attacked it with a hammer because he wanted to take the cuckoo out into the garden to sing on the lawn, but Lela had made such a fuss that he had not been able to carry out his project. But Lamia, for once, was completely unsympathetic, for Huda would be broken-hearted. She blamed Lela bitterly for ever letting him climb on a chair and get hold of the clock and then she picked up Moomi, spanked him hard, and deposited him with a thump in his cot. They all spent a miserable evening listening to his roaring and head-banging; he was a very persistent child.

Next day Moomi woke like a bright morning with no trace of a stormy evening and leaped into Lamia's arms as though there had never been a cloud between them. 'It's no good trying to teach him,' thought the girl wearily, 'he's too little to understand, and, anyhow, it was Lela's fault for not watching him . . . We'll go out for a walk, Moomi,' she added aloud. 'We'll go up the hill after breakfast to where the baby goats play behind the church.'

She had been so busy since returning home, getting the house to rights, coping with school and homework, that she had not yet had time to visit Amin's grave. But this morning she would go and, Moomi permitting, she would sit for a little time in the dim, incense-scented church, and look again at the figure on the crucifix, arms outstretched, wounded for her transgressions, bruised for her iniquities, bearing her load. She had been twice to Mass but she had not found the answer she wanted; there were too many people and too much movement. Perhaps there, by herself, if Moomi could be occupied with the baby goats, she would meet the Person she was reading about. Perhaps, there, she would learn to love and forgive.

It was a quiet day; not bright sunshine, but soft muted colours and clear horizons that heralded rain, and this was a good thing, for the fields were too dry for late ploughing. Here on the coast, the spring was much further advanced than in the mountains and scarlet anemones grew in drifts in the grass. Moomi trotted along, chuntering to himself, for he loved going places; anywhere, provided they were moving and on the way. He could walk quite long distances now and was growing sturdier every day. 'I'll put him in a kindergarten after the summer,' thought Lamia. 'He looks more than the proper age. I wonder how old he really is.'

Moomi made straight for the graves, for he had a special game of playing hide and seek with himself behind the tombstones and Lamia turned towards the church. But a young Maronite nun was just leaving, and she smiled at the hesitant girl. Lamia had always thought of nuns as aloof and unapproachable, but this young woman had a pleasant open face and seemed willing to talk. They sat on the stone parapet and she listened quietly while Lamia poured out her troubles and Moomi ran to and fro and presented them with hot little bunches of flowers.

'I know,' said the nun at last, 'My friend's fiancé was killed on the southern border in a clash with the Israelis and she entered the convent. There seemed nothing left in the world to live for, so she turned to the love of God.'

Lamia considered this statement. What she had read in Hanni's Bible had moved her to believe in the love of God, but there were still big, unanswered questions.

'The love of God!' she burst out rather bitterly; 'but tell me this, Sister, if he really loves, then why has all this happened? Why did her fiancé die? Why did my mother and brother die? Why this torment, if God loves? Why, oh why doesn't he stop it, and why is the world in such a mess?'

The young woman sat silent for a time. This was something she had often wrestled with in her own suffering and meditation, but it was hard to put her conclusions into words.

'I don't know,' she answered at last, 'but I think this: God created the universe to work in harmony when governed by the rules of love. But if we break the rules and choose another law, then everything clashes and the world is plunged into chaos. I think God works within his own law, not within the law we put in its place. He does not cancel the law of cause and effect . . . love is the medium in which he works to save; but the world has turned from love.'

'Then there is no hope,' said Lamia flatly. 'We are just a prey to other people's wickedness.'

'No; I think we still have a personal choice. In a world of war and hate, I believe that I can still submit to the law of love; then my life will be lived out in harmony with God.'

'But what do you mean? How do you submit to the law of love? Do you feel that you love God? I sometimes feel as though I hate him.'

'Yes, I know ... and yet, he never told us that our feelings are what matter. I think he measures our love only by our obedience; it's not how much do I feel, but how far will I obey?'

She spoke hesitantly, feeling for her words, and seemed relieved when Moomi interrupted the conversation, dragging at Lamia's hand to come and see a little river. He was very wet and had apparently fallen into the little river.

'Is that your brother?' asked the nun.

'No,' replied Lamia. She felt no need to pretend with this simple, clear-eyed young woman. 'We found him lying under his mother's body near our home. He's a Palestinian.'

'How do you know?'

'His mother fell not far from the camp, and besides, I recognised her clothing; besides ...' she stopped, confused, and the nun looked at her questioningly.

'Do you not know to whom he belongs?'

'No ... at least ... no, not really ...'

She knew that her voice was unnecessarily agitated, but she could not help it. Her new friend was still looking at her.

'I know,' she agreed gravely. 'We have many lost children brought to the Convent, and sometimes relatives come seeking for them. Sometimes it is hard to give back a child you have learned to love, but what joy it is to restore him to his true home. If relatives come asking for a little boy of his description, shall I tell them you have a child?'

'No,' shouted Lamia, losing control of herself, 'leave him alone! He's our child now; we're not going to give him to anyone.' She snatched him up and hugged him to her and he screamed and struggled and pulled her hair. The young nun laughed.

'I should think you have your hands full,' she observed. 'I am glad none of ours are quite so . . . er . . . energetic. Goodbye, Lamia, and God bless you; and, remember, I think that day-by-day obedience is the only measure of love God ever gave us. The Cross was simply the obedience of love.'

She turned away to go back to her work and Lamia put Moomi down. He ran off down the path and Lamia followed him. The idea that loving went along with suffering was somehow resolving itself into a trinity; love, obedience, pain — but productive, life-giving pain that sprang into deeper loving; the winter before the spring. She sensed that it was all leading her toward something that she could not face, and she stayed for only a short time beside the green, flowered mound that was Amin's grave before hustling Moomi home. She felt annoyed with him, because he had shamed her in front of that peaceful young woman, who had kindly called him energetic; but what she really meant was that he was abominably spoiled.

The sight of the broken clock depressed her still further and she sat for a time trying to find out if it could possibly be mended. She feared not; it had been so beautifully carved and made to respond to gentle handling and careful winding, and then it would have kept time and sung its gay little song for ever. 'But if we break the rules then everything clashes, and the world is plunged into chaos.' Yes, that nun had been right; you could not blame the craftsman, if Moomi attacked his handiwork with a hammer, that the bird would sing no longer; it had never been designed for blows and hammers. Love is the medium in which God works, and his universe was never designed to respond to bombs and guns and hate. These were men's choice, but they need not be her choice. Some day, one day, she would have to decide; but not yet . . . not yet.

15

Through the early days of March the fragile peace held, although strained to the utmost. While there was no official war, the radio spoke of almost daily kidnappings and killings, as any man with a gun now felt free to wipe out any personal grievance unchallenged. Up in the Bekaa there was a breakaway movement of the army under Moslem control, and Tyre and the South were defecting toward it. 'If the army divides,' said Elias sombrely, 'then any semblance of law and order will break up for good, and the madness will burst out afresh.'

But the young continued to hope and to pack every moment of life and freedom that they could into the hours of this so-called peace. It was good to walk in the streets and go to shops and visit your neighbours, even if your suburbs lay in ruins about you and your family was depleted by death. Spring had burst on the Middle East in its rich fulness, blossoms veiled the twisted girders, daisies, marigolds and blue bindweed made gardens on the graves. Hanni came back from the hospital one evening and came to call. But he greeted her gravely, suppressing his joy at the sight of her, for she still wore her dress of mourning. He came home very little, for the hospital where he worked lay to the west of the city and even now, in time of peace, no one passed from the east to the west, or the west to the east, unless they had to; besides, the hospital was still crowded out. But, for once, he had risked it, and he and Lamia sat on the verandah in the last evening light, talking. There was so much to tell, but at last there was a little pause and the girl's bright face grew sober.

'I read your Bible, Hanni,' she said simply. 'I liked it. I liked that bit about Jesus bearing our griefs and sins and dying instead of us, but . . . it's hard, isn't it? I mean, it makes you think you've got to do something, doesn't it?'

'Well, so you have. Love like that demands a response.'

'But what? What have I got to do?'

'I can't speak for you. Your problems are your own. But he is alive and active, and when you accept him into your life, you know . . . I think he shows us each our own particular path of love. Lamia, come with me tomorrow; we are going to meet in the house of the man I told you about, the man who came and talked to us in the shelter. I haven't been able to go for a long time, but quite a group meet there on Saturday afternoons, and it's not far from here. The roads in that direction are quite safe and we shall be back by sunset.'

'I'll ask my father,' said Lamia, and changed the subject, for she felt as though some strong tide was bearing her in a direction she did not want to go. And yet, she was curious to see this man who was neither priest nor monk, but who had brought such a change to Hanni. Beside, she was glad to go anywhere with Hanni on a fine Saturday afternoon in spring.

Her father made no objection. He felt vaguely that her life was too dull and house-bound, but he had no idea what to do about it. He was pleased to see her dressed in her best, firmly shutting the door on an angry Moomi, and setting off to meet her friend. Lela was likely to have a noisy and trying afternoon. Elias decided to go out himself and leave them to it.

Hanni met Lamia at the gate and they walked along the upper outskirts of the town, through the relatively safe Christian suburbs to the east of the city. They walked for about half an hour, not talking much but revelling in the sunlight and blossoming gardens, in the freedom of simply going somewhere together after the separation and confinement of the past months. They arrived all too quickly, thought Lamia, when Hanni stopped at the door of a white house and knocked.

They were a little late, and the room was already crammed with men and women of all ages, and even some older children. They welcomed Hanni and Lamia with enthusiasm and Lamia noticed that they all had Bibles of their own; she noticed, too, the air of expectant joy, as though they had come to meet a loved friend. When the greetings were over, they started singing to a guitar and the songs they sang were simple and easy to remember. Lamia thought the words came from the Bible; she liked the catchy tunes and was beginning to enjoy herself, until their host rose and opened his Bible.

Lamia stared at him. He was quite young and not very impressive-looking but there was something about him that made you listen to him. She had often heard priests talk about God, but this man seemed to know God personally. When he read, it seemed as though God was speaking, and the words struck the girl so forcibly that she heard nothing beyond them, although later, when she looked at her watch, she realised that the man had been talking about them for quite a while.

She was sharing Hanni's Bible and she sat staring at the passages, deaf and blind to all else, reading it over and over again. "If you love me, you will obey my commandments. I will ask the Father and he will give you another Helper, who will stay with you for ever . . . Whoever accepts my commandments and obeys them is the one who loves me. My Father will love whoever loves me; I too will love him and reveal myself to him. My Father and I will come to him and live with him."

Here it was again; love linked with obedience, involved with suffering. Yet in these verses the mists parted and you caught a glimpse of the beauty beyond the suffering; the presence of the Comforter, Christ, revealing himself to her, God, coming to make his home with her. She did not understand what it meant but it seemed like a shining, undiscovered country, lying just beyond the barrier of obedience. 'You will know your own particular path of love,' Hanni had said to her, and he was right. She knew what keeping the commandment would mean to her. The room suddenly seemed dark and close and the words swam before her eyes. To refuse was to lose the bright country ahead; to accept was to lose Moomi.

The talk drew to a close, and people prayed; but they were not praying to a dead figure on a crucifix, but to Someone who was there, alive and very near. And he was very near. 'All right,' whispered Lamia, 'I'll obey. I'll do anything you want, and I'm sorry,' and she knew that her hatred of the Palestinian woman, the lies she had told, and her mother's broken vow were all part of the burden that had been carried away. Her heart lifted and, for a short time, she seemed to have passed the barrier by an act of will and to be at home on the boundaries of the shining country. She said goodbye in a sort of daze, and she and Hanni walked home almost in silence, for the evening light on the flowered grass verges, the bright rim beyond the mountains across the bay, and the colours of the sea, glimpsed suddenly between battered rooftops, seemed not of this earth. Hanni, recognizing that her thoughts were too full for speech, said very little and when she reached her front door, she did not ask him in. She just smiled at him in a way he never forgot, and he went on down the hill, whistling.

But as Lamia entered the house, the brightness receded, as she found herself face to face with the stark reality of the next step. Moomi saw her, gave Lela a kick on the shins, and ran to her. She picked him up, and he twined his arms

133

round her neck, showered her with wet kisses, and looked into her face, his great black eyes soft and loving. He knew quite well that Lela was going to tell that he had been a bad boy, and had deliberately sat on the loaves she had put to rise, so he was getting in first and Lamia knew it. But he was hard to resist when he looked at her like that; she yielded to his wiles, hugged him unashamedly and felt that her heart was breaking.

But at this barrier she could not stand still; she must either travel forward or turn back into the mists of not knowing, the loneliness and the guilt. That, she knew now, she could not do, and what was to be done she had better do quickly. She carried Moomi up to bed and lay beside him for a long time, telling him stories, singing the little songs he liked best, until he fell asleep suddenly cuddled up against her. She disengaged herself gently and went downstairs to find her father.

Lela was in the kitchen, Sami absorbed in his homework, and her father sat reading the paper in the front room. She drew up a low hassock and sat at his feet. 'Father,' she said, 'I want to tell you something.'

He laid down the paper and gave her his attention, and she told him the whole story, omitting nothing. He listened in silence and when she had finished he continued to sit, deep in thought, for a long time.

'I am sorry, Lamia,' he said at last, and his voice was unusually gentle. 'You loved the child, and so did I, but we cannot steal him from his own, and, as far as we know, his father is alive as well as his grandmother. Besides, perhaps what matters most of all is, what is best for Moomi.'

'Best for Moomi? Surely it is best for Moomi to grow up here and become a Christian?'

'He was born a Palestinian and God orders our state in life. Besides, Lamia, have you not noticed? The child should not be here with us now that Rosa has gone. You

134

must get on with your schooling and Lela cannot control him, and I don't want to send her away when she has lost so much; but can't you see how spoilt and wilful he is growing?'

'But Father, the Palestinians are our enemies.'

'But not his enemies; you told me she was a woman of noble bearing. Did she look poor or hungry?'

'No, her clothes were of good quality. She just looked very tired . . . oh, Father!'

She laid her head against his knee and wept bitterly. He laid his hand on her hair and let her cry for a time. They had never drawn so close to each other before.

'Lamia, my daughter,' he said, after a while, 'let us not waste any more time. Where is that telephone number? Let us do this thing while the peace holds. If the fighting breaks out again, we shall not be able to meet her; it would be too dangerous. It may be now or never.'

Lamia listened as though in a dream, unable to believe that this thing was happening. There were certain preliminaries to decide, explanations to be made to the grocer in whose shop the phone rang, and then they could hear the sound of a woman's broken weeping and a voice praising Allah as Lamia's father issued directions.

'You must come to the spot in the orange grove where you found your daughter's body at eleven o'clock; you must bring the photograph. We will meet you with the child. If his father is there, he must come too.'

It was as easy as that, and, in another way, the hardest thing Lamia had ever done in her life. She slept little and woke at cockcrow; she lay staring at the paling window and the last stars, feeling as though some necessary part of her was about to be amputated. Moomi woke to a flaming sunrise and she lifted him into bed with her for a time, until he tired of her tears and kisses and shouted to get up. She washed and dressed him with great care, packed his clothes

135

and toys in a plastic bag, and wondered how to pass the last hours. It was Sunday and people were climbing the hill to Mass, but she did not want to be parted from Moomi, so she took him into the garden and played the games he liked best, until her father called that it was time to go and they walked slowly into the orange groves, each holding one of the child's hands.

They walked in silence down that path of vivid memories. It was the path down which she and Amin had run so gaily on the day of the birthday; here was the spot where his body had been laid and, a little further on, the place where the young mother had died. They were in good time, but the grandmother had arrived before them, and they saw her quiet, black-clad figure standing alone under the brilliant foliage from some way off. She did not come to meet them; she stood there, erect and controlled, her hungry eyes devouring the child, and a look that reminded Lamia of light and sweet music swept across her face as he came near and looked up at her, and she knew him.

She was standing in the right place and she handed Elias the photograph without so much as glancing in his direction. But she did not speak or move; she stood waiting, and Moomi stared and stared, and then drew back and nestled against Lamia in an uncertain sort of way. But he went on staring and, gradually, his eyes became bright and unfocussed as though he were seeing something very far away and long ago. And still no one moved.

And then the wonderful thing happened, and yet not so wonderful, because the parting had been less than a year before. He moved toward his grandmother and held up his arms. She stooped without haste and picked him up gently and he laid his head on her shoulder, stuck his thumb in his mouth, and never looked back. He had come home.

'Praise to Allah!' murmured the woman and, for the first time, she looked at Lamia, who was only a little younger than her daughter had been. The girl's face was white and her eyes washed out with weeping but she had not tried to detain him. Absorbed as she was with her grandson, the woman showed no sign of recognition. 'You loved him, too,' she said wonderingly, 'yet you gave him back. What love is this?'

But Lamia could not speak and she did not say goodbye. She turned away and started home up that path of sorrow. Only her father lingered a few moments and spoke to the woman before catching up his daughter.

'What did you say to her?' asked Lamia.

'I gave her our address. Moomi's father is still in Tripoli. If there is further trouble — who knows? She may be glad of it. Her house is right at the entrance of the camp, almost next to where Kamal lives.'

He put his arm round her shoulders and they walked home in silence. She felt very tired, but quiet and peaceful; and, stranger still, she could not remember feeling great sadness at the time of the take-over. Later on, the sorrow and longing would return full blast, but then she would also understand and feel glad that, for that hour at least, she had completely forgotten herself. She had been thinking entirely of Moomi, and, from the look on the woman's face and the vague, far-away brightness of Moomi's eyes, she had known that it was well with the child.

16

Perhaps it was the very uncertainty of the peace that made that spring so glorious. The radio still rumbled of mutiny and defection in the army and everyone knew in their hearts that it must all blow up again soon; but, in the meantime, in the city, the sun shone, the nights were quiet and every day was precious, as days are that are numbered.

For Lamia they were confusing days because of her mixed emotions. They were days of sorrow because of her bereavments, days of loneliness because Moomi no longer ran to meet her when she came into the house or slept beside her in his little cot. But they were also days of joy because the burden had been lifted and Christ had come to her. His Presence seemed to cast a new light over everything, brighter than the spring sunshine, or the colour of the flowers and the young grass. Never had the world seemed more fair or those she loved more precious. She found herself longing for Huda, longing for her grandparents, newly aware of her father and Sami, and even Lela wondered what had come over the girl. She had been so petulant and irritable but now she usually spoke gently and even listened to what the poor old woman had to say. Lela felt strangely rested and put it all down to the absence of Moomi whom she had considered the devil incarnate.

Lamia also knew that she was beginning to love Hanni. Nobody really thought that the present cease-fire would hold; the rumblings and rumours of war became more menacing every day. But if the guns spared them both, then she believed that, one day, in some distant era of peace, they would be married, and this was a steadying thought.

She was too emotionally exhausted to feel passionate or excited. Her love seemed to grow with the spring quietly and beautifully and without crises. For the first time since Amin's death she knew that, even against the dark background of bereavment, the light could shine again in the foreground.

Sami had not continued his training with the militia. His father had strictly forbidden it and Sami was surprised to discover how relieved he was to obey. War — to fight for your Christian heritage — had seemed so glorious, but now the glory had departed and only the scars and burnings remained; Amin's grave on the hillside, the memory of his mother's white, white face when they threw the earth on it, and Farid, lying on the dark hillside, screaming and blind; and no one, apparently, any the better for it. He felt cheated and disillusioned, and to turn back from a hero's life to being a schoolboy again was a dreary prospect. Lamia sensed his dull unhappiness and longed to comfort him, but he was silent and uncommunicative, usually burying himself in his books or kicking a ball idly up and down the garden.

He had missed more schooling than the others, and sometimes he would ask Lamia to help him. She was sitting beside him one evening in March explaining his French conjugations and she asked him a question. He did not reply, so she glanced down at him; he was sitting, staring out of the window at the froth of cherry and apricot blossom. He wasn't listening at all.

'Sami!' she gave him a little nudge. 'You're not attending. What's the good of me telling you, and you don't listen?'

He turned and looked at her and she saw that he had not heard a word of what she had said.

'When can we go back to the village?' he asked abruptly. 'Will you ask Father to take us?'

She shook her head.

'It's impossible; there is fighting in the mountains and the roads are not safe. Wait a little longer, Sami. I too want to go to the mountains and see Huda and the grandparents.'

'I want to see Farid. Lamia, do you think he's still blind?'

His young face wore a haunted look and she tried to speak cheerfully.

'I don't know. Perhaps the hospital cured him.'

'I don't think so. You can't cure blind people. I think he's still blind, just sitting there with nothing to do and nothing to see. You once said there was a Blind School; did you ever find out about it?'

'No; it's a dangerous area. But if peace holds and the schools open, perhaps Father would take us.'

'Thank you; if he could learn something it would be better, wouldn't it? Lamia, I wish you hadn't given Moomi away.'

Her eyes filled with tears. To talk of him was like probing a deep wound.

'So do I; but I had to, didn't I? It was stealing to keep him. He belonged to them. Besides, Mother promised.'

'But they are our enemies. He'll grow up a Palestinian and a Moslem. Is that good?'

She did not answer, because this was the question that kept her awake at night as she lay re-living that last walk. Moomi had returned to his own place; he had known, and he had not looked back. But he would grow up to fight and inherit the flaming hate and resentment of his displaced people. She would never be able to teach him that loving was the only thing that mattered, nor tell him what she had begun to discover, that when Christ was received he became a living source of love and forgiveness. She could do nothing more for him now, and he had so far to go.

She laid her arm across Sami's shoulders. 'I'll go and see about the Blind School as soon as we can,' she repeated, 'And now, Sami, do try and think about those irregular verbs.'

Her father was ready to help when she questioned him. He knew exactly where it was and told her a little of its history. It had been started by English Christians long before, and had grown with the years. During the bombing it had closed, but now with the current peace, it might well have re-opened.

'It's not far from Sami's school,' said her father, 'and they say the schools are about to open. Things are quiet there just now. I'll drive you both in tomorrow, and you can go and ask about Farid while Sami runs up to see if his classes are starting again and I'll park in the square and wait for you both. But no dawdling, mind! We don't want to stay longer than we need.'

They all set off the following afternoon. Lamia found the place easily enough and stood looking curiously into the little shop window where cane work was exhibited – beautiful chairs, baskets and trays, plaited by blind boys. Then she rang the bell and was admitted.

She was taken to a covered verandah looking out on a large playground, where a young woman was doling out supplies of flour and sugar to a group of sightless lads who seemed on excellent terms with her. The woman's name was Jamila, and she explained that the school had been damaged and had not yet re-opened, but, should the peace hold, the boys would return in the early summer; in the meantime, they came for regular food supplies and other care. When Lamia told her about Farid and asked if there was room for another, she shook her head slowly.

'There are so many,' she replied. 'We have just been asked to admit a girl from a bombed village; she lost her sight and her parents in one day. We have never taken girls before, but I think we should start. Another of our lads came down to enquire whether we were open, and he went back to his village to find his whole family massacred. So many have been blinded in the explosions, we don't know how to accommodate all who apply. However, it is not for me to say yes or no. Wait till the Principal's wife comes back. She has only gone to the shop and she won't be long.'

They chatted for a time until an older woman hurried into the courtyard. Jamila introduced her as the Principal's wife, and she listened while Lamia explained her errand, but her manner seemed agitated.

'We will certainly try and admit him as soon as we're open,' she said. 'Just keep in touch.' Then she added abruptly, 'Where do you live? How did you get here?'

Lamia told her.

'Then go at once,' she said. 'Go to where the coast road branches inland and try to get a lift from there, but don't try to get back to where your father's car was parked. Trouble has broken out again. They're shooting, and people are being kidnapped. Go quickly, while there is time! I would drive you but the traffic jams are so dense that it's quicker to walk.'

Lamia stood rooted to the spot. Kidnapping! And Sami would just be on his way home from school to meet his father in the town and get a lift home. But there was nothing she could do. She would never find him among all those frightened, fleeing masses, nor could she ever reach the town against that tide of humanity all surging in one direction. She said a brief goodbye and plunged into the street. As she left the building she could hear the not-so-distant crack of rifles and machine guns.

She was not afraid for her father. He had his gun in the car with him, and the meeting place was out of the centre. But Sami! Kidnapping was worse than shooting. So often the body was dumped in some waste place days later, as

Amin's had been, and no one would ever know what had been suffered in the intervening time. She was in anguish and her mouth was dry, but she pushed her way into the almost solid block of cars, tapping frantically on the closed windows, begging a lift. In the end she found someone going her way and crammed herself into a small car and sat on the lap of an old man, while the horns blared above the turmoil behind them and the traffic jams, piling up at the checkpoints, seemed doomed to stay there for ever. But somehow they were moving and as the roads fanned out on the outskirts of the town the traffic speeded up and within quite a short time she was put down close to her suburb. It was still light when she reached home, and, apart from old Lela nodding in the kitchen, the house was empty. She switched on the TV and watched a Brigadier of the Palestinian Armed Struggle Command making an impassioned appeal to overthrow the President, and announcing the formation of a new government.

Lamia was not impressed and switched it off. She had seen too many cease-fires and had, for the moment, ceased to care about governments unless they promised life and peace. Nothing really mattered any more except that her father had not come home and Sami was somewhere out there in the fighting and killing. Then a car stopped outside and she rushed to the door and opened it as her father hurried up the steps.

'Is the boy home?' he asked.

She shook her head and saw the colour drain from his face.

'I hoped you'd bring him,' she said. 'Could you not reach him?'

'It was impossible to get anywhere near the school. The traffic was just carried along. No one could turn, nor was it possible to walk against the crowds leaving the centre like ants from an ant-hill. I waited on the main road, but hoped he'd found a lift. I will go back into the town and see if I can find him.'

'Father, you cannot go back into the shooting. And if he's . . . all right, then he will have left the town.'

'Then I will meet him and bring him home; or else . . .'

'He wants to die with him,' thought Lamia dully, 'and what about me?' But aloud she said, 'Father, there are so many ways by which he could come. Wait a little, and let me make you some coffee.'

He shook his head and went off without a backward look and she was left alone, for Lela had gone to bed. It was beginning to get dark. She opened the window at the front of the house and the dusk veiled the graveyard but the warm spring air seemed pregnant with the ghosts of those who had gone; a laughing ghost that was Amin; a gentle ghost and a very small, merry ghost who flung fat arms round her neck; they were gone, gone, and now finally Sami and her father had gone too.

Gone where? Her straying thoughts seemed to focus on the question. Where were they, these dear dead? The church said they were in purgatory and she ought to be lighting candles and saying prayers for them, but she had not been able to face the thought of them in pain and had done nothing about it.

But where were they?

Memories came thronging back: that spring morning, nearly a year ago when she had woken at cockcrow and known that moment of unearthly joy. If that was the moment when Amin was shot, it was rapture he communicated, not pain. She remembered her mother's face, that same night, as she knelt, looking up at the suffering figure on the crucifix; 'You will know so much more,' she had said, 'but this I know; Christ died because he loved.'

Of what use was all that suffering, if they still had to suffer?

She switched on the light and sat down to re-read that first chapter that Hanni had showed her. "But because of our sins he was wounded, beaten because of the evil we did. We are healed by the punishment he suffered, made whole by the blows he received. All of us were like sheep that were lost, each of us going his own way. But the Lord made the punishment fall on him." And, as always when she read that passage, she remembered her mother's outstretched arms gathering all the hate and the bullets into her own body. 'But I am alive and well,' she thought. 'She took it all.'

And if he bore it all, what is there left for us to bear?

She switched off the light again and sat for a long time thinking. The sky behind the mountain was a blaze of stars, the scents from the garden rose like incense, and in her heart was the beginning of a wild, amazed hope. Her mother had trusted all along, and, surely, Amin, in those last days of terror, had found what he so earnestly sought for. If so, then was not the work of the Cross sufficient? And, in that case, had they not gone straight into the presence of God? She remembered that Christ had said to the repentant thief next to him on the cross, 'Today you will be with me . . .' That changed the whole face of death . . . if it was really true.

She was still sitting there, thinking, when the car drew up and her father seemed to drag himself up the steps, and she knew, before she even saw him, that his search had been unsuccessful. He slumped in a chair, grey-faced, and seemed unconscious of her presence until she brought him coffee. He sipped it absent-mindedly and stretched out his hand in her direction as though seeking some re-assurance. She came nearer and it rested on her hair.

'If he has gone,' he said at last, 'then that's that. Maybe it is better for a boy to die than to grow up in a world like this. But if he has been kidnapped . . . has he not known enough terror in his thirteen years? And we shall never know.'

She leaned against him, yearning to comfort him.

'Father,' she whispered, 'have some more coffee and let me cook you a meal. I think Sami is safe somewhere. I think God is out there in the gunfire . . . I think Sami will come home.'

'Did Amin come home?' he asked quietly. 'Was God there when your mother died? What is your faith founded on, Lamia?'

She could not explain; only the veil between life and death seemed very thin and death no longer the final tragedy. 'Today . . . with me'. Here or there, they would come home. But how could she make her silent, reserved father understand? She had never felt able to talk to him much but now, if there were only the two of them left, she had better try.

'Your mother believed,' he went on in the same even voice. 'She believed when they brought Amin home . . . She believed when we lay in that hell of a basement, waiting to die. But if there is a God, then why . . . why?'

His voice cracked and broke off and Lamia was silent for a time, for she had no answer to that one. But the thought of those hours in the basement reminded her of something else and at last she spoke hesitantly:

'Father, I don't know; but, about dying — do you remember, in the raids last year, when the people used to crowd in at sunset and we would all lie in the passage? Do you remember how stale the air used to become? — stinking wounds and dirty babies and clothes singed with fire and explosive, and the snoring and the groaning! Sometimes I used to think I was going to suffocate and I would creep to the door early in the morning and slip out into the garden. Never will I forget that first breath of cold, fresh air, the silence or sometimes the bird song — the cleanness and the first light over the mountains and the sudden sense of well-being! Father, I think that for a believer, dying is like that. I think God was there when mother died. I think he opened the door and she went through.'

He stared at her dully.

'For a believer?' he questioned at last. 'And who is to say whether Sami is a believer. And anyhow, what about purgatory?'

She was silent again, for since his mother's death she had concentrated on just keeping Sami happy, helping him with his lessons, cooking the meals he liked best, and she had never shared what she was learning. 'It's all wrong,' she thought to herself. 'We work so hard to teach them how to live, but we never mention the most important thing, how to die. If Sami comes back . . .'

There was the sudden sound of small, weary feet scuffling up the steps, and a hand fumbled at the door handle. Elias leaped to his feet and a moment later Sami, filthy, cold and gasping, was clasped in his father's arms; and Lamia, clinging to them, knew without the shadow of a doubt that the joy of the dead was all round them, merging with the joy of the living and there was no grey shadow of pain anywhere.

At first there was not much to tell. He had run behind a wall when the shooting started and had lain for a long time trembling and, according to the streaks on his dirty face, crying. He had stayed there until it grew dark and then, in a lull, he had crept out and begun to run in what he hoped was the direction of home. He had stumbled over a rubbish heap and smelt appalling and he had got badly lost. But in the end, he had come to a checkpoint and a soldier had taken pity on him and begged a lift for him, and he was very hungry . . . the story trailed off, and his father took him for a wash and a change of clothing while Lamia prepared a meal.

They ate and ate; and, warmed by food and hot, milky coffee, the events of the evening became more and more exciting and horrific and his own courage and skill more and more amazing. He was no longer a weary, frightened child, but a glowing hero who, by his cunning and valour, had outwitted the whole manoeuvre. His eyes sparkled and his chest expanded while his father and Lamia egged him on and laughed as they had not laughed for a long, long time. Their boy was safe home, dead and alive again, lost and found and they could have gone on listening and laughing all night. But —just at the critical point of a fantastic escape story, Sami's voice faltered. 'I'm so tired,' he said suddenly and, leaning his head against his father's shoulder, he closed his eyes.

Elias helped him to bed and Lamia cleared the supper and went to bed too, worn out by fear, suspense and joy. But she could not sleep for a long time, for the implications of her new discovery, if they were true, were almost more than she could take in. For if death was just a step into the presence of God, then her dead were not very far away; they, at home in the love of Christ, and Christ, shedding his love abroad in the heart that received him – then they were all closer together than she had dared to imagine, united in that all-enveloping love.

But was it true? She thought of the look on her father's grey face when he heard those shuffling footsteps outside; of his broken cry of joy as he drew his soiled, weary son into the light of the house. And would God, the Father of all fatherhood, do any less when his own children stumbled through the dark valley of death and stood at the gates of home? She thought not.

17

The shooting in the city was the beginning of the next phase of the war and the worst yet. The move to overthrow the President (leader of the Christian party) was followed by a call for his resignation which he ignored, so militia units, fighting all the way, advanced. Halting five miles from the palace, they bombarded it, and two nights later the President fled with his family and guards. When morning broke, there was nothing left to bombard but the great palace dogs and heaps of personal belongings.

It was a great victory for the Moslem Left and a grave defeat for the Christian Right. Lamia and Sami huddled miserably together and listened to a desperate appeal from their Party Leader — a last call to arms. 'Our people and our army are scattered,' he cried, 'our institutions are falling apart, and our land occupied. There is no parliament, no system of justice, no authority, no security and no freedom. Ruin and destruction spread over villages and cities, towns and mountains. I appeal to you all, men and women, to unite for the homeland. Perform your holy duty and fight for your homeland which faces disaster.' And this was no overstatement, for the Palestinians were fast advancing in the mountains, gaining ground in what had seemed safe Christian strongholds. It was beginning to look as though a Palestinian victory was a possibility.

'They are winning in the city, too,' said Sami sombrely. 'Lamia, if they win everything, what will happen to us?'

'I don't know. I suppose we should be given certain quarters where we should be allowed to live, provided we did what they told us. I think most Christians would try to leave the country; thousands have gone already.'

'Well, they've got the Holiday Inn,' said Sami, with a little shiver. 'You didn't hear about that, did you. You were down the garden, picking lettuces. It was horrible; they stormed in by night . . .'

'I know, you told me,' interrupted Lamia hastily, 'I don't want to hear it again.' The account on the radio had sickened her, and Sami, who always heard everything, had added more gruesome details. The 26-storey Holiday Inn was a Christian Party stronghold but it butted out into the Western Moslem quarter and fighting had been going on round it for months in a sporadic way. But this time experienced army officers had joined the assault and under cover of darkness the Palestinians had swarmed into the buildings, kicking open doors, flinging in hand-grenades and killing every one of their opponents. When it was over, the victors posed for photographs grouped round the headless body of one of their victims, while other bodies were hitched to jeeps and dragged through the streets to celebrate the victory.

It was the beginning of bitter fighting, the 'Battle of the Hotels' which was to end in the complete partition of the city. The Christian party retaliated for their losses by mortar bombing the buildings on the seafront, and this bombing continued for months. Any shells falling short landed in the densely populated areas behind them, and the victims tended to be the women, standing patiently in the food queues or the children, playing outside in the stifling heat of the city summer. People huddled in their basements and cellars; human remains lay in the street because no one would venture out to move them. Schools and shops were closed and the city more or less came to a standstill, while the senseless, indiscriminate bombing went on and on.

Lamia went into the kitchen and gripped the edge of the

sink to steady her jangled nerves. She felt she was coming to the end of her tether and could stand no more. If only they could get away somewhere, as thousands of others were doing, away from the continuous dull roar and the suffocation of fear. She saw her father coming up the path and ran to meet him. He still carried on an irregular sort of business and had just been up the road to take some cloth to a neighbour.

'Father,' she cried, 'can't we leave? Terrible things are happening in the city; how much longer can we stand it?'

He drew her down beside him, realising that she was at breaking-point, and Sami joined them. It was impossible to go to the mountains, for there was fighting on most of the roads, but overloaded planes, bearing panic-stricken families, were still leaving from the airport, and fleets of ships were crossing to Cyprus from the north of the city. He looked thoughtfully at his children.

'I could send you to Cyprus, to your aunt's brother-in-law's cousin,' he said at last. 'I think they would . . .'

'But Father, we couldn't go without you. Why can't you come too?'

'Because if I stop earning, how would you live? Besides, we have nothing for the future except what is vested in this big house. Our property is our fortune. If we leave, this house will be looted or occupied or both, and we shall never get back into it. I have not yet told you what I have just heard about Samira's sister who lived in a house further down, adjoining the camp.'

'What? Did Samira tell you?' Their strained faces broke into smiles, for Samira was a joke; a great brawny woman, whose stories lost nothing in the telling.

'Yes; her sister's husband decided they would go to Cyprus with the children, leaving his mother in the house. The old lady went down to the bakery one morning, and when she came back, a family from the camp had broken in and taken over. They would not let her into the house at all, not even to collect her property. The father of the family pointed a gun at her and told her to run, so she did. She is living with Samira now, and I must say I'm sorry for her. So you see, I have to stay; but if you want to go, I will try to make arrangements.'

'It's like the night when he told Mother to take us in the boat,' thought Lamia. 'But she wouldn't leave him and neither will I. Nothing really matters as long as we stay together.' Aloud she said, 'I'd rather stay with you, Father, but if Sami wants to go . . .'

'I don't,' said Sami hastily. He had not realised, when so much had been taken from him, how tightly he clung to his father and sister. But he suddenly knew that, apart from them, he would be mere flotsam and jetsam, a refugee who belonged nowhere. Perhaps, thought Lamia, this realisation of the importance of each other is one of the best things about danger. We don't know, until we are threatened, how much we love each other.

'I wish Huda were here,' said Lamia.

'And Moomi,' added Sami softly. They drew a little closer and smiled at their father. The tension was eased and Cyprus was not mentioned again.

Lamia, too, felt sorry for Samira who already had to cope with a family of cousins, whose house had fallen in on top of them, and two days later, when there was a lull, she emerged cautiously into the street and went to visit her. She found Samira in high spirits, and was brought into an extremely over-furnished, over-populated room, made to sit down, and served black coffee.

'I was really sorry to hear about your sister's house,' said Lamia. 'And to think that they have held all her property too!'

'They haven't!' Samira threw back her head and her fat sides shook with laughter. 'I went with a cart and we took it all back. We hardly have room to move now, but it's better than losing it all.'

The family, the cousins and the aunt, perched about the room on what looked like pieces in a furniture store, joined in the general hilarity.

'You took it back!' gasped Lamia. 'Why didn't they shoot you? And won't they shoot you now?'

'Let them try,' chuckled Samira. 'They will not come so far into a Christian quarter. My sister's neighbour dared say nothing, but she watched. One evening she sent her little boy running to say the father and the eldest boy had gone down into the camp and taken their guns with them. So I set off.'

'Did your husband go with you?' asked Lamia.

'No, no, he was afraid.' She jerked her hand in the direction of a small man who peered apologetically over the top of the armchair. 'I had a cart ready. I took my two sons; they were afraid too, but they did what I told them. When we reached the house I knocked. When they opened the door we pushed in. I too had a gun.'

'We have come for the furniture,' I said.

'You cannot have it,' they said.

'We have come to take it,' we said, and my son pointed the gun. Their men had taken their guns and they could do nothing but cry. We carried out everything – yes, everything. Last night they slept on the floor without blankets and today they eat on the floor, if they can eat at all, for they haven't a thing left to cook in.' She dissolved into further fits of laughter and the family with her. Only the older son protested.

'That's not true, Mother,' he said. 'You left blankets for the children and everything the baby needed.'

Samira looked slightly ashamed of herself. 'Oh well, the baby!' she conceded. 'I wouldn't want to hurt a baby. But the others . . .' Once more, mirth overcame her and Lamia

153

laughed with them all till the tears rolled down her cheeks. It was a merry visit.

The first blast of a new explosion warned her that it was time to go home. She reached the house breathless, still laughing, to find her father and Sami hunched over the radio. They beckoned to her to come and listen.

'The leaders of both sides have returned from their conference in Damascus,' said her father. 'They are discussing peace proposals. Unless they can agree, the Syrians will invade. They have massed their tanks and troops on the border. It sounds as though they may find a way to agree.'

'Peace!' thought Lamia to herself. 'If the fighting stops, Hanni will come and visit me.' She gazed out on the mountain in blossom and thought she had never before seen it so beautiful.

On April 1st a new ceasefire was announced, although some said it was only a ten-day freeze to plan the next phase of the war. But, in any case, the fighting died down and people emerged from their cellars and basements, drew deep breaths, and began to clear up the rubbish and hold mourning for their dead, while others hoped afresh and watched for the return of loved ones. And on a beautiful April morning Hanni arrived, bright-eyed and unharmed. He came marching up the path beneath the apricot blossom and she saw him before he saw her, and because people said that peace had come, she knew that she now dared to let herself love him. Her joy almost lifted her off her feet, but she controlled herself, arranged her curls and walked to the door.

'Praise God I got across,' he said a little breathlessly. 'Peace or no peace the sniping goes on. But I wanted to see you so much that I risked it.'

She blushed and looked down for she was not yet ready to tell him how much she had wanted to see him. She was the child of a modest, reserved country woman, and her mother's influence was strong.

'Have some coffee, Hanni,' she said quietly, 'and then let's go out. Let's walk up to the church and sit in the sun.'

He smiled as he waited. He had seen the blush and he was not disappointed. He liked her quiet ways unspoiled by the free-living manners and influence of the western world. A banked fire burns longer than a roaring blaze and he wanted their love to last for ever. As they sipped their coffee, he told her about the past weeks at the hospital. The shortage of staff had been terrible as so many doctors had left the country and, because their hospital lay in the western quarter, nurses living on the other side of the dividing line could no longer travel to and fro. Those who remained seldom left the premises and lived at gunpoint like everyone else.

'They often control us with their guns,' said Hanni rather wearily. 'Sometimes we have to deal with three hundred shrapnel wounds in a day, and we try to make them wait their turn while we treat the more serious first. But when a group of Palestinian commandos bring in a comrade, they rush him to the front, waving pistols and threatening to pull the pins from their grenades if we delay. So there is nothing to do but to attend to him and woe betide us if anything goes wrong! One day, a fighter died on the operating table and, rather than face his friends, the surgeon changed in the theatre and left by the back door.'

He chuckled, but Lamia could see the strained look in his eyes. 'Let's go up the mountain,' she said. 'It's so lovely to be able to walk without fear and who knows how long it will last!'

'Don't be too sure,' he said sombrely. 'Eighty-five people were killed in the first twenty-four hours after the cease-fire. They have got into the habit of sniping and they can't stop.' Nevertheless, as they climbed the hill they forgot about the war and thought only of themselves and each other.

Lamia lingered, picking flowers as she went. It was the high tide of their blossoming just before the months of drought set in. In those early April fields, every shade of colour washed against each other – cyclamen, pale and deep pink, crimson anemones, great white daisies, starry pink asphodel, blue lupins and mauve wild hyacinths. The colour and scent was all part of her happiness and she was absorbed in it when he suddenly asked her a question:

'Where's Moomi? I didn't see him down at the house.'

She looked up. 'No,' she said quietly, 'he went back; come and sit on the terrace under that fig tree and I'll tell you all about it.'

So she told him all about it; the way she had accepted Jesus' love and given herself to him after the Saturday meeting and her decision afterwards; the meeting with the grandmother and the great emptiness that followed. And he listened with growing gladness, for if she shared this living faith that had so revolutionised his life, then he saw no further obstacle to their future together.

'You did right,' he said when she had finished, 'but I'm sorry. It must have been very hard.'

'Yes ... and yet somehow, deep down, I'm happier. Over the past weeks, since the schools closed there's been more time, and I've been reading that Bible you gave me, and I'm learning lots.'

'What are you learning?'

She glanced up the hill to where the grave lay hidden by a row of cypress trees. She hesitated and toyed with her flowers.

'Tell me.'

She smiled up at him. 'I've been learning about the dead and about dying. They seemed so lost and far away. I kept

156

reading that first chapter you showed me in Isaiah, and it struck me that if Christ really carried it all and we are made whole by the blows he received, why should we suffer as well? Surely, when we die believing in him, he counts us forgiven and welcomes us?'

'Yes, I suppose so; yes, I think it must be so.' Hanni's reasoning had not carried him as far as that, but then he had not lost his own flesh and blood.

'And then, you see, they are not very far away, are they? I mean, they with Christ and Christ in me, so the more I know Christ, the nearer we all are; as though they had gone on into love and I'm beginning to love; oh, I can't explain, but I'm learning so much more about loving.'

'And so am I,' thought the boy, looking at her flushed, animated face and the shadows of the young fig leaves on her hair. But he only said, 'What are you learning?'

She sighed. 'I don't know how to say it,' she replied. 'I'm just finding out that it's true what Mother said when she died, "Nothing else matters."'

18

In spite of a hazardous meeting of Parliament and the decision to elect a new President, everybody knew that the situation was rapidly getting worse, and even a new President could do little because the old President refused to resign. Yet in the face of certain Syrian invasion if fighting continued, the twenty-seventh cease-fire was announced in the middle of April against a background of heavy mortar barrages and once again, the shattered nation hoped.

But there were still those determined to continue and a few days later fifteen Christians were murdered as a reprisal for nine kidnapped and assassinated Moslems, and all Bedlam broke loose. All parties were determined to avenge their own wrongs, and the city gradually divided into separate, self-governed Christian and Moslem quarters; which was in a way a good thing, for at least people now dared to creep out into the streets and clear some of the huge piles of stinking rubbish. In the interval, householders had attempted to burn their own and learned to live with the sour, acrid fumes. It was a part of the way of life.

Sami, when he managed to escape from the house during a lull, kept arriving home with kittens. The cat population was exploding on the enormous rubbish dumps and lean kittens were ten a penny. They were, on the whole, a good thing, for they kept in check the equally exploding rat population and Sami could not resist them. Lamia and Lela scolded him sharply but he retired into the garden with them and hoped that out of sight was out of mind. Even though food was getting desperately short, his kittens comforted him and he gladly shared his meagre rations with them.

There, on the outskirts of the suburbs, it was a little easier to get food as the country people would creep to the edge of the town with barrows of fresh vegetables, eggs and chicken, and they asked what prices they liked. Also, in the garden, plums, apricots and first figs were beginning to ripen. They cut down a tree and, as the summer wore on, Sami became expert at bonfires, for the electricity was often cut off. Water, too, was a problem and households often had to queue at one main tap in the street. And meantime the weather got hotter and hotter and destruction and decay rotted and stank in the drought.

More and more people died and numbers ceased to mean anything as new and terrible weapons appeared on the streets, and the aiming was often at random and quite inaccurate. Ten little children died when a shell landed on a kindergarten and fifteen adults, when another landed on a cinema queue. But nothing could be done about it, and the remaining population, numbed with so much horror, was absorbed in the increasing problem of how to live through the next day.

But things had to get much worse before they got better, and people continued to flee the country like rats from a sinking ship. Then on a series of glorious days in June the airport was closed again after repeated bombings, the murder of the American Ambassador hastened the withdrawal of nearly all foreigners, either by sea or in long convoys round the dangerous southern roads to Damascus. The country seemed left in desolate isolation to finish its own destruction.

To begin with, Lamia, like everybody else, had lived almost glued to the radio, when it was working. But gradually the daily strain of living and longing made her almost unresponsive to what was going on, for, somewhere down in the city, in the middle of the missiles and the guns, Hanni was working, and there was no post, no telephone and no news. If he had been killed and his body pushed, with a number of others, into some common grave, she would never know about it. Her love had grown gradually like dawning light, but now she realised, for the first time, how total would be the darkness if that light was quenched.

The days were long and hot, and as Sami turned to his kittens for comfort, so Lamia turned to her Bible, finding in it strength to go on and a growing sense of nearness to the One who had suffered and experienced total loss and death. Death was no longer the dark end, because he had gone through and opened the door to whatever lay beyond, and her way ahead was to get to know him better. "Whoever accepts my commandments and obeys them is the one who loves me . . . I too will love him and reveal myself to him." So throughout the noisy, terrifying, imprisoned days she sought to love and obey, to keep cheerful for her father's and Sami's sake and to comfort poor, trembling old Lela in spite of her own heavy heart; and she had no idea how much they were all coming to lean and depend on her.

Then, while the eyes of the world were at last turned on Lebanon, while the Arab countries conferred and bargained and the new peace-keeping force marched in, while Christians and Moslems themselves continued to break up into small, factional parties, a new horror erupted which, for Lamia and her household, brought the holocaust nearer home. With things at last going their way, the army of the Right gathered together for a last mighty attempt to destroy the strongholds of their enemies and surrounded the camps on the east of the city.

Lamia thought mainly of the battle raging round the great camp below the orange grove, for somewhere in that blazing hell was little Moomi. The siege started in June and, although few reports got out, the conditions, in the

160

heat, were soon rumoured to be unbearable, and the thought of her bright little boy haunted her day and night. She pictured him hungry, thirsty and sick, and one precious letter from Hanni which he managed to send by hand did nothing to alleviate her fears. He told how, with great courage and diplomacy, the Red Cross had managed to send an ambulance into the camp to bring out those most critically wounded, and their reports confirmed all the rumours. One by one, the wells in the district were becoming polluted and dysentery had broken out on a large scale, while lack of food, medicine, water and sanitation was turning the whole place into a stinking, scorching death trap. Bodies were buried by night in a common grave, while a sheikh chanted the Koran in a whisper so that the sound would not attract the firing.

There was little to do now except to wait; to wait in endless queues for small rations of food; to wait her turn at the street tap for her buckets of water; to wait in the basement for the end of the bombardment; and to wait in the lulls for the new attack to begin; to wait through the hot, noisy nights for the dawn; and to wait through the scorching day for the slight coolness of evening. But during these days when Hanni and Moomi were seldom out of her mind she discovered the Psalms and started using them as her own prayers. 'Keep them as the apple of your eye, hide them under the shadow of your wings ... deliver them from their enemies, oh my God, and save them from men of blood.'

It was nearing the middle of August and, from all accounts, the Christians had stormed the camp and the siege was over. Sami, who heard everything, and who, during the lulls, seemed to go everywhere, had returned in a state of great excitement, for now, surely, the great bombardment would cease and their enemies be wiped out for ever. But Lamia was not excited; would Moomi die, or would he be found again this time under the body of his grand-mother? And if so, would anyone bother? Or would he share the fate of hundreds of other babies and little children?

And yet, what was the fate of these little ones? A few bewildered hours or moments of desolation and pain, and then they were home for ever, healed and made perfect, with the mad, hating, murdering world of war behind them. They would never hate, or fight, or weep; they would grow, in that medium of love, to their perfect fulfil-ment. All through the hours of that day she was deeply aware of the nearness and joy of her dead. The noise was deafening, for a Christian sector was firing from the south of the suburb but it seemed to recede as the day wore on and, that evening, as Lamia stood watching the polluted, smoke-dimmed sunset, she felt a kind of weary peace stealing over her. She prepared a meal for her father and Sami from what odds and ends she had been able to salvage and then went and lay down on her mattress in the basement and was soon fast asleep.

It must have been hours later when she was woken by a soft knocking. She raised herself on her elbow and looked at her father and Sami asleep beside her. It was quiet now, and it seemed a pity to disturb them so she slipped on her dressing gown and went to the window on the first storey above the front door, and, keeping well sheltered, she opened it a crack and called 'Who's there?'

Three figures stepped out into the moonlight: a boy, who carried a gun in his left hand and seemed poised for flight; a woman, who lifted her hands as though in beseeching prayer, and a little child, who stood quietly looking up at her and there was no mistaking that small, valiant figure, who waved weakly when he caught sight of her. All caution forgotten, she ran to the door and a moment later, Moomi was in her arms. She would have held and hugged him for a long time but the woman pressed forward. 'Let us in, my daughter,' she whispered through dry lips. 'Let me explain and then I will go my way. I have brought you the child; there is no one else left to care for him, but if they see us, they will shoot.'

She almost forced her way into the house and shut the door behind her. The young man disappeared.

'Give me some water,' gasped Moomi. 'I'm thirsty.'

She sat them in the living room, lit a candle and fetched food and water.

'Where is the young man?' she asked. 'Who was he and is he safe?'

The woman shook her head. Her face was strangely white and she seemed to breathe with difficulty.

'I think he will be shot,' she said simply. 'We live on the outskirts of the camp and when your people broke in this morning and started shooting, we hid behind a hedge of thorns in the grove. Kamal lives next door and he knew your house and he knew of your love for the child. He has lost his right arm and is blind in one eye and he cannot fight, but he showed us the way through the grove. Now he will try and escape to the west but I do not think he will succeed. Your people will spot him. They are killing without mercy.'

Kamal! He had come right to the door, and Lamia suddenly had a wild desire to face him, although whether to kill or to forgive, she hardly knew. She ran boldly out into the garden. The boy was still there, crouching in the dark shadow of the gatepost, plucking up his courage to slip out into those deadly streets.

'Kamal,' she said.

He leaped round, jerked his gun into position and his finger seized the trigger. But when he saw that she was unarmed and in her dressing gown, he dropped his gun to his side and tried to cover his poor scarred face with his hand. He was trembling all over, but he did not ask for mercy and they stood irresolute for a few moments, both torn by conflicting emotions, not knowing what to do or say.

He broke the silence. 'I brought you the child,' he mumbled.

'Yes, so I see. Thank you. What are you going to do now?'

'I don't know; I shall try to get to the west.'

Amin seemed close beside her, not cold and dead, but laughing as he had always laughed. 'It doesn't matter any more,' he seemed to be saying: and her mother, peaceful as in life; 'Loving, forgiving; nothing else matters.' She drew· a long breath.

'Do you want a drink of water, Kamal?' she asked.

He peered at her as though he was seeing a ghost. His face, or what was left of it, was ashen.

'Water? Oh yes, I think I'm dying of thirst. There was no water all day. But don't let your father see me.'

She brought him water and some cold macaroni and stood there while he gulped them down. 'You had better go,' she said at last. 'It's beginning to get light over the sea and if they find you in this quarter they'll shoot. If you go to the bottom of our garden, there's a lane down to the main road. You may make it. I can't spare much water, but here's half a bottle.'

He turned to look full at her with his seeing eye, his fierce pride struggling with his fear and misery. Then, as he turned to go, he whispered 'asmahle', which is the conventional, everyday word for 'excuse me, pardon me'.

And Lamia gave the correct reply, 'msmoh', 'pardoned', and went back to the house with a light heart; for now she knew, at last, that she had no enemies at all.

19

She closed the door softly and tiptoed back to the living room. Moomi, who had drunk deeply and eaten a little, had already fallen fast asleep with his head on his grandmother's lap, and Lamia gazed down at him for a full half minute. He was very thin and filthy dirty, his beautiful curls matted with dust and dead grass, his eyes sunken with dehydration. But he was whole and unwounded and hers and she stooped and kissed him softly. Then she turned to the woman slumped against the wall, drawing her breath with difficulty.

'Are you ill?' asked Lamia. 'Would you like to lie down?'

'Let me rest a little,' said the woman humbly, 'and then I will go. We escaped early this morning when the great shooting began. As your people stormed in, it seemed as though thousands of our people tried to run out. Whole families, men, women and children, were shot as they ran and fell in heaps together. I was shot, but did not die and Kamal, who lived near to us, was kind to us. He loved the child, whose father was killed in the siege three weeks ago, and he dragged us behind a hedge of thorns on the out-skirts. We waited all day without food and water but God be praised there was a little shade. At nightfall we crept through the grove and Kamal showed me the house. I have brought you the child for you loved him and here he will be safe. I . . . I am soon going to my Maker. It does not matter if the Christians shoot at me, for I think I am dying in any case.'

Her story had been punctuated by fits of painful coughing. Now she pointed upwards and struggled to rise, but sank back exhausted.

'You can stay here,' said Lamia. 'No one need know. Where is your wound?'

The woman pointed to her side and drew back her clothing. It was stiff with caked blood and between her ribs was an ugly, blue wound. The bullet had almost certainly pierced her lung and to get hold of a doctor in a hurry, at this point, was almost an impossibility. Lamia had no idea what to do, but Lela was experienced in sickness and suffering; perhaps Lela would know what to do.

It took a long time to wake Lela and a still longer time to explain the situation but, once she understood, she suddenly seemed to come into her own. Bullet wounds had been commonplace in her family and she had nursed her own son through much the same condition. Lamia watched, amazed, helping a little when required, as the old woman washed the wound and changed the soiled clothing with the utmost gentleness, murmuring words of comfort and endearment. 'It's very queer,' thought Lamia. 'Lela was always growling about the Palestinians, but I suppose this woman is just a sick patient now, and nationality has ceased to exist. Anyhow, its very clear that Lela's bark is worse than her bite.'

It was almost harder to explain to her father why they should, at this point, be harbouring a sick Palestinian in his house, but when he saw Moomi and heard the whole story, he shrugged his shoulders and agreed to her staying, although Sami was strictly sworn to secrecy. The radio blared the glorious victory and the bombardments ceased while, in the unaccustomed silence, Aisha lay dying, for the bullet was deeply embedded and, although Elias had gone to seek for medical help, it seemed unlikely that he would find it in time.

Lela sat beside her all day, ministering to her, and Lamia washed and fed Moomi and brought him to lie on her bed so that she could feel him near her, for he was weak with dysentery and hunger and had no wish to run about or play. Aisha's temperature was rising and, in spite of her breathlessness, the fever seemed to loosen her tongue. Sometimes she lost count of time and place and was back in her own country; back in Palestine, a happy young woman of noble birth, before the Israelis had destroyed her town and shot her husband in front of her. She had come to Lebanon as a refugee, fleeing with her little children and they had grown up in the camp. But one by one the guns had got them, and now there was only Moomi left. But every time her eyes rested on him, a look of profound satisfaction settled on her face.

'Our people are stateless, fugitive. They have no country, and the world will not receive us. But he will have a home . . . he will be loved . . . he will have a nationality and a country . . . he is yours . . . he will know peace . . . God has had mercy on him.' She murmured the broken sentences from time to time, but as the day dragged on, she became more and more breathless and talked less. Lela sat beside her, bathing her face, supporting her, giving her sips of water, and Lamia came and went. That evening, when she had put Moomi to bed, she too came and sat beside Aisha in the dusk and, after a time, she fetched her Bible and read the verses she had only recently discovered; 'I am certain that nothing can separate us from his love; neither death nor life, neither angels nor other heavenly rulers or powers, neither the present nor the future, neither the world above nor the world below – there is nothing in all creation that will ever be able to separate us from the love of God which is ours through Jesus Christ our Lord.'

She thought that Lamia was reading from the Koran, which pleased her. But that universally understood word, that knows no frontiers, that transcends race and colour and that breaks down all barriers, reached her. 'The love of God,' she whispered, smiling, 'and the child . . . you loved him . . . you will always love him . . . promise you will always love him.' And Lamia, without the slightest hesitation, promised.

Aisha died very early next morning, at cockcrow, with Lela, still awake, holding her hand. The rest of the household slept on, unused to the strange quietness and when they woke she was ready for burial, and the air was already swimming with heat. Elias and Sami and a couple of neighbours dug a grave on the hillside and they buried her facing the sunrise, as she would have wished. Lamia did not go with them to the burial. She stayed at home with Lela and Moomi and when Moomi was told that his granny had gone away, his mouth went down at the corners, his eyes filled with tears, and he lay for a long time in Lamia's arms, quiet and apparently staring into space. But he accepted it, as he had accepted all the other changes and violence and sudden deaths in his short life, and by evening he became a little more lively. Lela, who had so rejoiced at his departure, seemed suddenly devoted to him; but then, there was no doubt he had returned a different child, tamed and submissive and strangely loving.

There was still some mopping up to be done, and the inevitable sniping continued, but people began to realise that it was coming to an end. The heat was intense, the rubbish and the ruins still sweltered and stank, but, as the days passed, water flowed in the taps again and lights went on in the houses. The summer drew to a close, the pomegranates ripened, and the leaves in the vineyards turned gold and crimson; then the first rains fell and, almost overnight, wild crocuses sprang up on the hillside straight from the blood-stained bullet-ridden soil, and the

thin green haze of new growth fell like a veil over the coun-
tryside. But minor battles still raged, the schools remained
closed, and people stayed near their homes waiting for they
knew not what. For many, life would never really start
again. The estimated forty-four thousand killings and one
hundred and eighty thousand woundings had left too many
scars. They might rebuild broken homes, but broken hearts
are not so easily mended; and, bitterest pill of all, no one
appeared to have benefited from the price paid.

It was a cool day in November, with early rain showers,
when the Syrians, with a thirty thousand strong peace-
keeping force, marched in and took over the country. In
some political circles there was anger and suspicion; in
others there was joy. But the ordinary man in the street,
satiated with horror and bloodshed, welcomed them
unashamedly. Peace had come, for a time at least; now they
could sleep quietly in their beds and visit their relatives. The
shops would open, and the children would play outside.

Elias and Sami had gone to see the celebrations, but
Lamia sat on the steps in a fugitive gleam of sunlight, trying
to take in what was happening. Moomi brought a few toys
and climbed quietly into her lap, his body pressed against
her, communicating warmth and growth, and her own
body felt alive and vibrant, as though quickened by hidden
springs. Hanni would come, perhaps today, and she
thought that they would get married very soon now. His
father had managed to retain his business right through the
war and she hoped that Hanni would finish his studies and
re-enter the hospital as a medical student, but that was up to
him; Huda would come home and life would start again.
The power of renewal felt so strong within her that she
knew, for sure, that one day she would bear Hanni's
children, but no child of her own would ever be more
deeply loved than the sturdy baby lolling in her lap; not the

fruit of her womb, but the fruit of her anguish and conflict, her forgiveness and victory, and therefore miraculously, inseparably part of her forever.

Rosa seemed very near, as though life had come round, full circle through the seasons, to another spring. Lamia was glad that she and Hanni, unlike their parents, had known each other before marriage. Their love might never strike deeper roots, but it would be more confident, more articulate and satisfying in the early years. She was glad, too, in a vague sort of way, that they had shared in the universal suffering, for they would always be more compassionately conscious of the dark pools of fear and hate lapping on the very threshold of the sanctuary of their own home.

She seemed to see her home as a tiny watershed in the wilderness. God was the source of love, pouring himself out in Christ, seeking access, usually denied, but here and there finding an entrance in a heart open to the Holy Spirit. Then the love overflowed through channels of dedicated service, happy homes, and children brought up to prize tolerance and goodwill above all other riches. Then everywhere the river came, life and healing would spring afresh; green grass would cover the graves; marigolds and morning-glory would make gardens in the bomb craters, and living waters would well up in the desert. Rosa was right; love was the only path to peace and nothing else mattered.

Moomi suddenly gasped, swivelled round on her lap, seized her nose to make her look in the right direction and pointed with a grubby forefinger.

'Look,' he shouted, 'there's two!'

She turned and they watched together. The sun had broken out again and a great double rainbow hung over the ruined city. It was so wide, so clear, so radiant in its promise, it seemed to span the whole of the coastline from Tyre to Tripoli.

971253
2014

⊃38

F.19